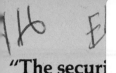

"The securi... what we're doing up here."

Robin's protest, made in a voice husky with passion, was far from convincing. She could have happily stayed forever in the deserted office with Jay, but the feelings he aroused in her were too intense, unsettling.

Jay smiled gently and sat down on the edge of his desk. The way his trousers pulled taut across his muscular thighs was almost Robin's undoing.

Drawing in a shaky breath, she tried again. "We can't stay here, Jay."

"You're absolutely right." Grinning seductively, he ushered her toward the elevator. The doors closed. With one arm Jay pulled Robin's willing body to him; with the other he pressed the emergency stop. . . .

Cindy Victor and her husband, Gary, are "empty nesters"—and loving it! Now that their two wonderful children are grown, Cindy is happy keeping her romance with Gary thriving, tending her California garden and being a full-time writer. Her articles appear weekly in newspapers throughout California and Nevada, and her short stories have appeared in numerous literary reviews. But Cindy says she has the most fun writing romances.

Books by Cindy Victor

HARLEQUIN TEMPTATION
  60–AN INTIMATE OASIS
138–KINDRED SPIRITS

Kindred Spirits

CINDY VICTOR

Harlequin Books

TORONTO • NEW YORK • LONDON
AMSTERDAM • PARIS • SYDNEY • HAMBURG
STOCKHOLM • ATHENS • TOKYO • MILAN

For Gary,
because the honeymoon cruise
to Hawaii never ended.

Published January 1987

ISBN 0-373-25238-2

1

"ROBIN! ROBIN, DARLING! Oh, my dearest!"

Robin felt loving arms wrap around her and she hugged back, hugged tight. Opening her mouth to speak, she surprised herself by sobbing instead.

The woman released Robin from the embrace and with tears in her own eyes, held her at arm's distance. "Oh, Robin, you are beautiful!" she cried. "Oh, my darling, let me hold you again! You can't know how happy I am!"

Robin found her voice at last and half laughing, enjoying the pleasantly perfumed second embrace, she responded, "I'm just as happy! Hello, Mother!"

They both laughed then, looking at each other a bit self-consciously, a bit in awe of the moment. Caroline Lasalle was as lovely as Robin had known she would be. And in her birth mother's eyes—eyes she had never looked into before—thirty-one-year-old Robin Alyse Eagle saw a glow of pride.

"All through the years, I had a mental picture of what you would look like," Caroline said happily.

"But I didn't imagine we would be so much alike! You have my eyes!"

Robin laughed again. The wide clear gray eyes weren't all that she'd inherited from this gracious, smartly dressed stranger. "I have your cleft chin, too," she said, scrutinizing Caroline's face unashamedly.

"Yes, but thank goodness I gave you only a small cleft! My aunt Helen—*your* great-aunt Helen—has more of a cleft than any woman could possibly want! Oh, Robin, I can't look at you enough! You look so like me when I was your age! Do you tan easily? And do you dance well? Do you usually sneeze in the morning?"

"Yes, yes! And *every* morning!" Robin affirmed, linking arms with her newly met mother. She felt completely at ease in the Honolulu airport, as if she'd been met by a dear old friend. It was a situation she had never contemplated in earlier years.

Robin had always been able to accept the fact of her adoption without trauma. Her parents, Eleanor and Ken Eagle, had been all that she—or Caroline—could have hoped her parents would be. Satisfied with the family she had, and knowing herself to be well loved, she had never thought to go looking for those people whose blood she shared.

Of course there had been times when she was curious, especially in her teens. Then she would stay up late wondering if her mother was beautiful, if she was very wealthy...maybe even famous. She wondered, too, if her mother was happy, too happy to be bothered with the memory of a baby she'd given away.

It hadn't occurred to her back then that her birth mother could be happy and successful and still think about her a lot.

"Do you know, Robin, that I said a prayer for you at least once every day of your life? I always said, 'Let her be well and happy, God.' It was the first thing I did every morning. Honest—even when I overslept!"

Robin smiled and patted Caroline's arm. "It worked," she assured her. "I've been well and happy almost all my life." That statement wasn't exactly untrue, she rationalized. She was blessed with good health. She'd had her share of emotional pain, but she always bounced back. It was her firm belief that most experiences were good ones, and life would only be boring if it exceeded a few hundred years. This attitude she shared with her mom, who'd seemed as excited about this trip as she was.

Eleanor's prediction that this trip would be one of the most momentous experiences in Robin's life had been right on target. Now Robin was glad that fate had conspired to get her to Hawaii.

She had recently had a medical scare when a routine test had been switched with that of another woman. The mistake had been quickly discovered, but it left Robin wondering about her genetic history. Some medical problems ran in families. If either of her birth parents had heart trouble or high blood pressure, or any other weakness that she might inherit, she felt strongly that she should know about such potential problems.

It was then she decided to make contact with Caroline. It seemed logical to seek out her birth mother, as her birth father might not even know of her existence. And even if he did, Robin wasn't sure she would feel comfortable contacting him. Just finding the woman who had borne her would do for a start.

Once Robin began to search, finding Caroline was a snap, as Eleanor had said it would be. Hers had been a privately arranged adoption, with Eleanor and Caroline sharing the same gynecologist. He had referred them both to a lawyer specializing in adoption. Although the Eagles had never met the biological mother of their daughter, they'd signed legal papers that had both birth parents' names on them.

Some years ago Eleanor had told Robin these as well as the doctor's and lawyer's names. "You don't think you want to meet them now, Robin, but you might some day," Eleanor had said prophetically.

The day had indeed come, and Robin had been spared the arduous search that so many adoptees went through. In fact, when Caroline had asked about that during their first phone conversation from Oahu to Las Vegas, Robin had assured her that she'd had more trouble locating her slippers on some mornings.

Face-to-face at last, mother and daughter had so much to talk about that Robin hardly noticed the hubbub of Waikiki, followed by the exquisite views afforded by the Lasalle home's fortunate location.

When Caroline stopped her BMW in front of her estate home on Diamond Head, though, Robin took note of the setting. "Caroline, it's lovely... just heavenly."

Since initially addressing Caroline as "Mother," Robin hadn't called her anything. The emotional scene at the airport aside, she felt that "Mother" and "Mom" should be reserved for Eleanor. Eleanor hadn't had to share those titles with anyone else during the past thirty-one years, and Robin didn't think she should have to now.

Caroline's smile conveyed her understanding and agreement with the choice of her first name. "Thank you," she said. "It is lovely, isn't it?

"We talked about moving into something smaller, but George loved this place and he couldn't bear to part with it. It's hard to keep up a house this size, even with full-time help indoors and out. Sometimes I long for a smallish condominium, but now that George is gone I feel I should keep the house out of respect to his memory. I wish you could have known my husband, Robin. George Lasalle was a wonderful man."

"I wish I could have, too," Robin replied in all sincerity. She was certain that anyone Caroline felt so strongly about would have to have been a special person.

"Besides, I want a big place for grandchildren to come and visit," Caroline added, opening the car door. "I *do* want grandchildren!"

Robin was taken aback. How odd for Caroline to have said something so personal; even in the short time Robin had known her she felt it was out of character. And that she embodied Caroline's only hope of having the joy of grandparenting was the furthest thing from her mind right now.

She was Eleanor's only hope for grandmother status, too, but Eleanor had never verbalized her hopes to Robin. Too well, she knew Robin's feelings about letting love enter her life, and if she didn't agree with Robin's attitude, at least she respected it. Well, Caroline would have to learn to respect it, also.

After introducing Robin to Mailia, the Portuguese-Hawaiian housekeeper, Caroline showed her to her bedroom suite. Besides exquisite furnishings and a vase filled with fresh flowers, there was an original Monet on the east wall.

Murmuring her appreciation of the painting, Robin looked forward to a leisurely examination of it later. Right now she was too excited to give it the admiration a masterpiece deserved.

Strolling outside to the terrace, which overlooked the azure Pacific, Caroline apologized, "You must be exhausted from the trip. And from my questions. It's just so tempting to try catching up on thirty-one years in one afternoon!"

"I'm not tired, and I have just as many questions to ask you, Caroline," Robin replied with a smile. "I thought I just wanted to know the basics—things like what countries my ancestors came from, does anyone in the family have diabetes or glaucoma. But now I want to know things like . . . like . . ."

Caroline helped her out. "Like do I tan well, and do I love to dance. And do I sneeze in the morning?

"Exactly!" Robin laughed, then luxuriated in a deep breath of the freshest air she had ever known. Actually, having lived all her life in Nevada, she hadn't had much opportunity to smell a sea breeze.

"Well, please ask me anything you want to know," Caroline prompted. "I'm showing no restraint in delving into your past, so feel free to do the same with mine!"

But there were some things Robin knew she wouldn't ask. If Caroline ever wanted to talk about why she gave her child up for adoption, she would. Robin also wouldn't ask if her birth father even knew of her existence. That was something she now felt she wanted very much to know, but to ask would be to invade Caroline's privacy.

No, she would keep to medical questions and be satisfied to find out the odd bits of family trivia. Already she knew that Great-aunt Helen had an enormous chin cleft.

Robin's thoughts were interrupted when Mailia came out to the patio. She served them iced tea with succulent wedges of lemon straddling the tall glasses' rims, then unobtrusively left.

"I hope you're comfortable," Caroline said. "This isn't the most body-pampering outdoor furniture around. When George picked it out I had something else in mind, but this was the look he liked. I suppose I could change it now . . ."

As Caroline let her sentence trail off, Robin found herself thinking that, though Caroline had loved her husband, she had been almost completely dominated by him. And George Lasalle's dominance hadn't ended with his death. How sad that a woman wouldn't buy comfortable patio furniture just because her husband had liked the look of something else.

Despite her thoughts, Robin assured Caroline that she was perfectly comfortable. And it was true. Although the white metal chair was hard, she felt wonderfully at ease. This sky, this vast sea before her, Caroline's splendid home—all contributed to the good feelings she was sharing with the woman who sat next to her.

"Ahh, my darling Jay is here!" Caroline exulted. "I would never confuse the sound of his car with another. I swear I could recognize that engine in a storm! It was George's car. Oh heavens! Robin, I've been so excited I didn't even tell you about Jay! Forgive me!"

Robin still didn't have any idea who Jay was, and Caroline didn't elucidate.

"My darling Jay." Robin frowned slightly, thinking that with all Caroline's talk about George it would be strange for her to have a boyfriend.

She found herself smoothing the skirt of her comfortable and cool black dress. Its short sleeves were cuffed boldly in winter white and a wide white V insert down the front emphasized the perfection of her breasts and narrow waist. Finger-combing her shoulder-length strawberry-blond hair, she thought wryly that this was certainly a new experience, meeting a mother's beau. Eleanor, also a widow, had never dated anyone seriously.

Robin suspected this man would look similar to George Lasalle, of whom she had seen pictures. George had been tall, handsome and distinguished looking, silver haired, somewhat older than Caroline. And now she knew he'd been outgoing, affectionate and very domineering.

This Jay person would have to have a lot of qualities that Caroline found attractive, to compete in her affections with George Lasalle's memory, Robin mused. Just at that moment the French doors opened. There, a sardonic half smile on his face and one eyebrow cocked quizzically in Robin's direction, stood darling Jay.

"Jay, I'm so glad you're here!" Caroline beamed at the imposing, sun-bronzed, golden-haired man.

He was, Robin decided, much closer to her age than her mother's. Flustered, she stood up to offer him a handshake. Jay enfolded her fingers in his, but ignoring her original intention, he embarrassed her by leaning down and kissing the back of her hand.

"So you're the Robin visiting the family nest," he said smoothly, straightening to look down at her upturned face. "It's good to meet you, Robin. I'm the Jay."

"Oh, you!" Caroline laughed. "I knew you'd make a joke about names! Well, Robin knew you were 'the Jay'! I told her when we heard the car!"

Turning to Robin, Caroline added, "It's a Rolls-Royce. It was George's, as I think I told you. Good grief, I'm so excited this afternoon I can't remember what I've said and what I've left out! But Jay loves the car."

I just bet he does, Robin thought, quickly extracting her small hand from the two large ones that had casually imprisoned it for too long. She knew she hadn't imagined the caress of those hands, nor his amber eyes raking over her body with the swift appraising gaze of a man appreciating what nature had bestowed on a woman. The sensuality of this greeting, especially from a man who was her mother's lover, was in excruciatingly poor taste.

Robin nervously touched a finger to the white earring at her lobe, a gesture that surprisingly brought a more sincere smile to the overwhelmingly knowing eyes peering down at her.

"Caroline does that sometimes," he said.

Robin smiled back and used Jay's comment as an excuse to turn her attention to Caroline. She couldn't understand how someone like Jay—a user, a gold digger, a gigolo if there ever was one—had come into Caroline's life. That he was Caroline's lover was apparent. When he stopped by Caroline's chair and bent down to give her a peck on the forehead, her hand came up to caress his cheek in a gentle, loving gesture. "Mmm, I love that cologne you wear," she said.

Robin was so unhappy about this turn of events that it was difficult not to show her feelings, but she knew that for Caroline's sake she must keep her opinion to herself.

Jay was studying her again. As he was still standing, while she had reclaimed her chair, he had the advantage of height, and she felt dwarfed by his perfectly proportioned six-foot-plus frame. The unstructured tropical suit announced muscular leanness, and his crisp pin-striped shirt covered a chest that Robin knew instinctively was impressive. He rocked back on his heels just a bit, and when he did Robin couldn't help but perceive powerful thighs straining against the expensive cloth.

Realizing with horror that she was mentally undressing him, Robin attempted to take firm command of herself, but she couldn't seem to regain the sense of well-being she had enjoyed before Jay had arrived. She couldn't ignore his ironic smile or his keen eyes any more than she could ignore his intimidatingly sensuous body.

He seemed to be amused by her being there, but he also seemed wary of her presence. Robin decided that if she read him correctly he was thinking: *So, you're the daughter. Now state your business. Why are you here?* Under his callous exterior, he probably felt guilty as sin, wondering if she was there to rescue Caroline from him. She wished he would simply disappear.

Jay sat down so that his broad shoulders blocked the better part of Robin's view of the horizon. A breeze as harmless as Caroline's untroubled gaze moved wisps of Robin's and Jay's hair simultaneously. While Robin nervously tried to calm the errant strands, Jay, his fingertips forming a contemplative steeple in front of his perfect bronzed jaw, didn't bother. That his attention was riveted on her and not Caroline nearly made Robin sick with discomfort.

"This is so lovely! You get a nice sea breeze up here, don't you?" Robin observed, biting her tongue for chattering so inanely. Before Jay had come tooling up to his lover's splendid home, in George Lasalle's Rolls-Royce, everything she and Caroline had said to each other had seemed meaningful—filled with warmth and the happiness the day had brought to them. What a shame to have it ruined. Most of Robin's concern, however, was not for her own discomfort. It was for Caroline—poor, vulnerable Caroline, who had fallen into the clutches of this gorgeous rat.

The gorgeous rat, not deigning to comment on the lovely sea breeze Robin had just complimented, continued to regard her over the tops of his fingers. Without moving, he caused more of a physical change in Robin than the hair-ruffling breeze had. She blinked, feeling her heartbeat speed up and her color rise. To her absolute mortification her stomach complained of the tension with a loud rumble.

Caroline, thank heavens, picked just that moment to speak, and no one could hear the embarrassing grumble except Robin. Mothers always came to the rescue, Robin thought, turning her grateful attention to Caroline.

Apparently unaware that neither her lover nor her daughter were ecstatic about each other's presence, Caroline said, "I'm delighted Jay could get away from the office this afternoon. You don't know how rare that is, Robin. Since he's been at the helm of Lasalle Engineering, he hasn't had as much time for me as I'd like. But I admit to being greedy on that score. I try to find ways to trap him for a few hours."

At the helm of Lasalle Engineering! Robin was finding Jay more morally repulsive with each new nugget of information she learned about him.

He chuckled at Caroline's admission to craving his company. In a self-satisfied drawl if Robin had ever heard one, he replied that he would be around a lot more during the next two weeks. And he said it while looking at Robin. She was suddenly as miserable as a tourist who'd come to Hawaii for the sunshine, only to find there would be unrelenting rain for two weeks.

"I wish you could take a vacation, starting right now." Caroline looked adoringly at Jay.

I wish I could go home, Robin thought miserably.

"I couldn't do that, but I might surprise you with how much I'll be around. You might get tired of seeing me," Jay jokingly warned Caroline.

"Never." Caroline promised, laughing at the preposterousness of that remark.

The obvious meaning of Jay's comment caused Robin to cringe inwardly; she hoped the flush of anger she felt wasn't showing. Not for the world would she ruin Caroline's happiness at having this . . . this poor excuse for a man here. But what gall! The arrogant so-and-so had taken over George Lasalle's business, his car and his widow, yet he wouldn't show Caroline the decency of refraining from an interest in her daughter.

Under the Eagles' tutelage, Robin had grown up and lived her adult life trying never to judge people. It couldn't always be helped, though. The two men she had loved and placed her trust in, she would forever judge severely. But ordinarily she had a live-and-let-live attitude. Okay, Caroline had a gorgeous lover much younger than herself. Robin had him pegged at about thirty-four or thirty-five. He gave Caroline affection and she gave him wealth. So what? It happened all the time. Nobody had to get hurt.

In this case, though, somebody would. And that somebody wasn't going to be *darling* Jay. Robin could see that Caroline was a trusting person, not blessed with the cynicism necessary to escape having her heart broken by such a man.

She wondered if feminine vulnerability passed between generations. She had been burned twice, and poor Caroline must have loved the man who had made her pregnant and then hadn't married her.

"I'm almost afraid to ask, but will you be able to have dinner with us at Canlis tonight?" Caroline asked Jay. In an aside to Robin, she explained that he worked late more nights than not, then added, "I suggested Canlis because it's your favorite, Jay. And if you do come, remember that it's to be my treat."

"Sure, love to. But only if it's my treat, Caroline. And it is," he drawled, looking steadily at Robin, "going to be my treat."

Robin smiled insincerely, hoping he picked up on her true feeling. She no longer felt sorry for prejudging someone. It wasn't the December-May relationship she was judging here; it was Jay. If he could look at her the way he did, and hold her hand in his as he had, and make such insinuating comments, he wasn't deserving of Caroline's love.

He wasn't deserving of any woman's love, come to think of it. Robin decided that she would relish the opportunity to tell him that to his face.

"We accept your kindness, sir." Caroline said happily. "I'll go inside and call for our reservation."

But before Caroline could get up Jay stopped her, saying, "Don't bother. You stay out here with our lovely Robin. I'll call." As he passed Robin's chair he touched her shoulder. Shocked by the brief contact, she dreaded seeing awareness dawning in Caroline's eyes. She needn't have worried, though. Caroline, who must have seen the inappropriate intimacy, didn't look at all perturbed.

Apparently she was blind to what he was, but Robin felt it wasn't her place to try to open her eyes to him. She wasn't there to rescue Caroline, or to interfere. The fact that Caroline was her birth mother made it difficult to ignore the woman's plight, however. She had only to think of how she would react if this were happening to Eleanor.

It wouldn't happen to Eleanor, Robin realized with a sigh. Her fifty-eight-year-old adoptive mother was much too levelheaded for any playboy to wrap around his finger.

And of course a man like Jay wouldn't give a plain woman like Eleanor the time of day. Using a beautiful wealthy widow whose days were spent in a Diamond Head mansion was definitely more in keeping with the habits of a gigolo than was becoming involved with a hardworking paraplegic in Las Vegas whose life revolved around plants.

"I've never been back to Las Vegas," Caroline said, as if Robin had transmitted the thought. "My parents moved away from there shortly after I came here to work. Anyhow, I love it here! I can't imagine living away from the ocean. It becomes so much a part of your life. Do you think you would like living by the sea?"

Caroline's tone had been light. She wasn't sad about never having gone back to the place where she'd grown up, fallen in love and had a baby, and she wasn't suffering from any awakening knowledge about Jay. It was just unbelievable to Robin that Caroline was in such a good mood, that she couldn't see her lover for what he was.

"I guess I would like it," Robin answered. "But it won't ever happen. I'll have to be contented with occasional vacations by the ocean. But the infrequency will make me appreciate it all the more when I have it."

Caroline smiled and nodded. "Then I shall appreciate it all the more when I have you here. Did I tell you, Robin, that I always loved you? And that I'm more proud of the woman my baby girl became than I have been of anything else in my life?"

Overcome as she was by emotion, and unable to speak, Robin's answer was found in her brimming eyes and her gentle smile.

The poignant moment ended with Jay's reappearance. He didn't touch Robin's shoulder as he passed her this time. Unaccountably she felt a stab of disappointment and despised herself for it. She despised him much more, though, and pleaded with destiny that he be too busy at the office to spend much time there during her visit.

But whether she had to see him a lot or not, she would worry about his hurting Caroline. This wouldn't be a temporary concern, either, one that she could blithely forget after she went home. Caroline was no longer a stranger about whom she fantasized. She was real, and to be cherished.

Jay's voice broke in on her reverie. "Robin, why don't you take a swim? I'm sure you'd find it refreshing after your trip."

Caroline quickly chimed in. "Why don't you two take a swim together?"

"That's a great idea! I don't know why I didn't think of it myself." Jay was out of his chair before he'd finished speaking.

"I don't think I'm ready for a swim yet," Robin hastened to assert. "I'd rather just relax and talk with you, Caroline. But go ahead, Jay. Don't let me stop you."

He sat back down. "When you're ready, we'll do it," he drawled, and Robin felt the double entendre was like a slap across the face—Caroline's face.

2

FORTY MINUTES LATER Robin was in an oversize pool with Jay. First she'd been adamant in her refusal. Then, at Caroline's urging, she'd said yes, though she did think it strange that the older woman would want them to be alone together. She had a bleak moment, wondering if Caroline really did know that Jay was a gigolo and just accepted his behavior.

But then Robin assessed the situation differently. Caroline was just so blessedly guileless herself that she expected the people she dealt with to be uncompromisingly forthright, also. She didn't see that Jay was flirting with her daughter, because she herself would not flirt with anyone.

Despite having to have Jay in the pool with her, Robin was enjoying her swim, which seemed a balm to her troubled nerves. From the moment she broke the pool's bracing surface with a crisply executed dive, she had to give Jay credit; this definitely took the kinks out. Effortlessly she swam underwater to the pool's shallow end.

Swimming was Robin's only sport. She was extremely good at it, having grown up with a pool in her backyard. During the painful times—when her father died and her mother had been crippled in a highway accident—Robin swam for therapy. Then she swam for her high school's glory. And at nineteen, when her trusting heart was given a swift kick by a University of Nevada punter, she smoothed the rawness of her heartache by swimming as much as three hours a day.

But now the nursery consumed most of her time. She didn't have spare hours for swimming. Still, the body remembered. She had good muscles, good lungs and good form. But best of all, during the moments she was gliding through the water, she had a respite from Jay's presence.

"Beautiful dive, Robin."

"Thanks." She smoothed the hair off her face and flattened it behind her ears. Jay had been in the deep end when she dived, but he'd gotten to the shallow end first.

"You have great form," he said appreciatively. "You really do know what you're doing all the time, don't you?"

Robin looked at him. It had started out as a simple enough compliment, but it hadn't ended that way. There was mockery in the gleam of his amber eyes. It was subtle, but it was there. As was her inner response to his attractiveness.

It wasn't as though she wanted to react to him. He was contemptible, really—beyond the pale. Yet his facial features, his lush blond hair, darkened now by the water, and everything nature had blessed him with from the neck down had an almost hypnotic appeal to her. She did not know which of them was appraising the other more intently, but suspected that she was the culprit.

Not wanting to be thought rude for staring, Robin grasped for some accompanying conversation. "How many laps do you usually do, Jay, to get the kinks out? And what is it about Lasalle Engineering that causes kinks?" Silently, she answered her own question—he was probably over-employed, which would no doubt be stressful.

"Actually, I don't do laps. In the ocean it's too far to the other side and back."

He grinned and, moving a step closer to Robin, lifted a strand of wet hair off her cheek and tucked it behind her ear. "There. Okay, Robin. You look like you wish I was doing laps in the Pacific during a killer storm. I'll just do the length of the pool, though, if you don't mind. I could use fifteen for the Lahaina project on Kauai, and fifteen more for the Talafofo Falls Hotel on Guam."

And he left her at the brightly tiled edge of the shallow end so she could wonder in solitude what in heaven's name was going on with her. Even as he swam away, she couldn't help watching him. The perfect bronze body slipped through the water with ease, and Robin knew he wouldn't be winded at the end of his thirty laps. If she didn't stop looking at him, though, she would be.

She turned deliberately and looked up at Caroline's graceful home. It wasn't difficult to understand George Lasalle's inability to part with it in his lifetime. On the other hand, if Caroline could take charge of her life and sell the house, she might be able to rid herself of Jay, also.

Robin held on to the pool's edge and leaned her head back, letting the late afternoon sun caress her throat with its shimmering rays. She closed her eyes, then opened them in renewed appreciation of what they beheld. The clear sky was what blue was always meant to be but seldom achieved. Where the brilliant sun kissed this privileged spot of Earth, the scent of both sea breezes and Caroline's breathtakingly exotic flowers mingled.

Jay's breath was suddenly near Robin's ear. Very near. He had come up behind her without so much as rippling the water. Either that or she had been so mesmerized by the idyllic setting that she wouldn't have known if a torpedo were coming toward her.

He put his hands on her waist. Robin shivered, feeling nearly faint. *Don't*, she begged him silently, but not a word passed her lips. Then his hands came around to her abdomen and he laced his fingers there, as if he and she were lovers and resting his hands against her flat belly were the most natural thing in the world to do.

She gasped and pulled in her stomach as tightly as she could in a futile attempt to escape his intimate touch.

"What are you doing?" she demanded hoarsely, her voice barely above a whisper, though she felt like screaming at him to get away from her. She was riddled with shame for not having spoken sooner. The time that had elapsed between his touching her and her demanding to know why wouldn't have escaped his notice.

"Nothing. I'm resting. With you."

If he was amused, Robin couldn't hear it in his voice. But her shame or his amusement weren't important at all. He was Caroline's lover, her business partner. His role in Caroline's life was much more important than Robin's. Therefore he had to be tolerated, but only up to a point.

After removing his hands from her waist with her own, Robin said a trifle tartly, "You hardly deserve to rest, Jay. What happened to the thirty laps?"

"I don't know about those laps," he said slowly. "I guess I got a yen to hold you on this one." With that, he lowered his body sufficiently to press his knees against the backs of hers, and Robin found herself half seated against his strong muscular thighs.

"You . . . ! You . . . creep! You disgusting loathsome vile degenerate *thing!*"

He let her go on *loathsome*.

When she whirled to face him, to let him know by her fuming gaze as well as the accelerating verbal attack just what she thought of him, she saw a quizzical look of amusement on his face.

"I could smack you!" she informed him between clenched teeth. "I could and I should!"

"Okay, okay." He backed away from her, raising his hands in the common gesture of surrender. "You don't have to say another word about it. I'll *do* the other twenty-six laps."

Robin was still sizzling in the water after he had deftly executed twelve lengths of the pool. She was as angry with herself for tolerating and even enjoying the initial physical contact as she was with his behavior. The compounded anger made her want to get out of the water, but she wasn't going to run away from him.

She stood with her hands on her hips, glaring as he approached her in the shallow end and departed for the deep. He reminded her of a shark.

"I did them all, ma'am. Am I forgiven my earlier laziness?"

"Very funny. You know damned well why I was mad!"

He whipped the water from his face, then stood close to her with his hands on his hips. "Robin, I'm a little concerned that you might be mad, in the literal sense of the word. What's bothering you? I'm sorry for what I did, making you upset. But for crying out loud, it can't have been the first time a man has come on to you. Not with your body and what it can do between the end of a diving board and the surface of the water. And you've got a solar-energy smile when you're not out for blood."

"I think *blood* is the key word here," Robin said, nearly stammering, she was so enraged.

"What do you mean? I swear, I'm in the dark."

Unable to restrain her fury, Robin let loose. "What do I mean? Just that if Caroline weren't my birth mother, I might be able to convince myself that what you're up to is none of my concern! I'd probably conclude, despite my disgust, that Caroline's a grown woman, capable of managing her own life, and that I should stay out of it. But she isn't just some woman I met for the first time today! She's my *mother*! And she obviously isn't capable of managing her own life, thanks in part to having been married to a domineering man. And when her gigolo lover comes on to me, I think it's past time for me to get involved! In other words, you'd be wise to consider your actions carefully or you'll force me to tell her what's going on!"

When Jay responded to her outburst with a full-bodied laugh after a few seconds of amazed silence, she cried, "What's the joke, blast you! Share it, if it's that good! Are you laughing because you don't think Caroline will believe me? She might not, but then again she might. Are you sure you want to risk it?"

Robin clamped her mouth shut and just stood in the water, waiting for him to say something. The only response from him that she would accept would be a promise that he would back off. And he had to mean it and leave her strictly alone. The last thing she wanted was to get involved in this sordid mess. Nor did she want to hurt Caroline, even if hurting her would ultimately help her. Who was she to say that Caroline shouldn't enjoy the company of this creep as long as she wanted it?

Jay was ruddy with mirth and his eyes were glistening with tears of laughter. "Oh, Lord," he gasped. "You thought . . . oh Kamehameha's ghost preserve us! Wait . . . let me introduce myself properly. . . something I should have done earlier! I, baby stepsister, am Jeremiah Lasalle, Caroline's stepson. The only lover that grand lady inside the house has had in the last twenty-eight years, to my knowledge, is my father, the late, domineering George Lasalle."

Robin's mouth fell open.

"No, don't be embarrassed. He *was* domineering, but that wasn't exactly unusual in his generation, Robin. That a husband should always get his way used to be incorporated in the Constitution and engraved in every bride's wedding band. Now, since I'm out of the gigolo category, can we shake hands and make up? Or do I have to do another thirty laps first?"

Robin was so relieved that she sighed audibly. It was half a groan of embarrassment, though, and Jay grinned at the sound.

She didn't mind. The chagrined smile slowly suffusing her face, despite coming in the wake of fury, gave way to a brilliant smile when she realized just how relieved she was. She held out her wet hand.

"The way you came on to me still puts you in the category of warty toads, but I'm . . . I'm happy to meet you, Jeremiah Lasalle," she offered.

This time Jay didn't kiss her hand. He shook it, then clasped both of his over it and drew her fingertips up against his wet chest. "I'm glad to know you, Robin Eagle. Listen, I hate being a warty toad—it's disgusting. Perhaps if you'd kiss me I'd become a prince?" He gave her a hopeful look. Though he had taken one of his hands away, the one that still held hers captive moved slightly against his chest.

Robin experienced an electric response to the feel of smooth skin, damp hair and the firm musculature of a man whose prime would last long and be glorious. She felt all this with more than her nerve endings, for the sensations seemed to pulsate right down to her quickening heart, and lower.

Determinedly, she reminded herself she didn't want any of this to be happening. In an attempt to lighten the moment, she responded to his glib invitation. "Oh, there must be some advantages to being a toad. Really, don't become a prince just for my sake. Savor being an amphibian."

Jay grinned. "I'll bet that when you were a little girl you caught toads and kept them in your jeans pockets. They never had it so good again, after you set them free."

"Yes, well, I've given up that hobby," she assured him. His playfulness might have been amusing if what he was doing to her hand hadn't set up a reverberation throughout her body. Besides, her throat was too dry for laughter, and she had to swallow hard before speaking. "I do apologize for the unwarranted hostility, for my words and most of all for my presumption. I . . ."

Jay's smile lit his eyes and it looked as if another bout of laughter was imminent.

"I should have known better," she admitted sheepishly. "It was crazy. Jay, I'd appreciate it if . . . ." But it was gutless to ask him not to tell Caroline about her shabby suspicions. And, after insulting him so blatantly, she didn't have any right to ask a favor.

"What would you appreciate?" he asked when she didn't finish her statement.

"I'd appreciate it if you let go of my hand now," she said.

"You sure?" he asked softly, but as he spoke he decreased the pressure of his fingers over hers. Then her hand rested on his chest of its own accord, with his fingers trailing idly over her wrist and to her forearm. She shivered, but nodded. His fingers retraced their gliding trail. Robin didn't take her hand away.

"Don't be afraid," he murmured, his tone as gently hypnotizing and seductive as his hand. "Warty toadism isn't catching. You may safely touch me."

"Thanks." She was a little breathless from the exertion of merely staying on her feet. The scent of his cologne had not been completely eradicated by the chlorinated water, and there was still a bracingly crisp smell about him. His breath, too, as he stood close and looked down at her, was clean and sweet.

With her back against the pool's edge, Robin couldn't move away. But even had she been in the middle, she wouldn't have wanted to distance herself from him.

At last Jay squeezed her hand, then let it go. A long second passed before she took her newly freed hand from where it rested on his chest. Extremely self-conscious about that small time lapse, Robin reverted to groping for conversation. "It really is a coincidence about our names, isn't it? I wonder if Caroline was reminded of me when she became your stepmother, because of that coincidence."

"Did Caroline know your name was Robin? I thought adoptive parents did the baby naming themselves." He sounded genuinely interested.

Robin gladly pounced on the nonthreatening topic, explaining that her case had been different from the majority of infant adoptions—there had been a link of sorts between Caroline and Eleanor, and Caroline had chosen Robin's name.

"My parents knew that having Robin Eagle as a moniker would earn me some teasing in school, and it did. But I was named out of respect for Caroline's sacrifice. It wasn't really that bad, either, except the year I had Bob White in my class."

Jay chuckled appreciatively.

"Tell me how you came to be called Jay. Jeremiah is a wonderful name. Don't you ever use it?" Robin asked, satisfied that the sexual tension had evaporated.

"Well, for one thing, I couldn't even spell it until I was nine, and by that time Jay had stuck."

"How old were you when Caroline married your father?" Robin asked curiously.

"Six. You know, Robin, it wasn't too swift of you to think I was Caroline's lover," Jay chided her gently, tweaking her chin with his fingers as he did so. "Let's keep it between us, shall we? Caroline might not find it as amusing as we do. She feels that she buried that part of her life with her husband, and she assumes everyone realizes that she did."

When he touched her nose, Robin found herself welcoming the brief intimacy, and she was more than grateful for his suggestion. Caroline would not be amused. "It makes me feel like an idiot to have thought that, even for a second," she admitted. "I'm usually not that much of an ass, Jay."

Her head was tilted back and she was gazing up into Jay's eyes as she spoke. Having criticized his father, Robin decided she should now mention that she knew how much in love Caroline and George had been.

Before she could speak, though, Jay startled her by asking, "What about you, Robin? Do you have a lover?"

"No!" She laughed at her quick, loud response. Then she decided that the passing on of such vital information should be mutual. "Do you?"

"I don't, and right this minute I couldn't be more glad."

She was slightly amused at the implication of his words, and her unspoken thought as she chuckled and shook her head was *No way, Jay!*

"A boyfriend, then?" he asked, smiling as if he anticipated her again saying no.

She obliged him. She didn't have a boyfriend. She didn't want one. Getting rid of the one she'd had had been like getting rid of a disease. She was unentangled and emotionally healthy, and, no matter what contrary message the media tried to drum into her, she knew she needed a boyfriend as much as she needed a hole in the head.

"Well, the damnedest thing about not having a lover," he said slowly, putting his hands gently at her waist, "is that you never know when the status quo will change."

"Look at my hair," Robin told him. "What do you see?"

Looking curious, but without gazing anywhere except at her gray eyes, he answered, "Slightly wet perfection."

"Well, Jay, when I'm white and bespectacled, when old Robin has crows-feet galore, then *maybe* I'll be ready to change the status quo."

Jay took his hands from her waist, nodding solemnly at her words. His gaze swept her brow and hairline and he reached tentative fingers to the skin beside her eyes. "Wait a minute," he finally said, scrutinizing her eyes and then her hair again. "I think...yes, I think that in this light I see silver. No, it's white! And I feel...aha! Little baby crows-feet. They're so tiny you can't see them, but you can feel them." Then his hands were on the back of her head, and he was leaning down to kiss her.

"Don't," Robin murmured. "I don't want—"

It was the last thing she said before he kissed her, his hands moving down her neck and back, caressing, lingering a moment at her shoulders, but gliding to their natural resting place below the water, below her waist.

By the time he was cupping her buttocks to bring her closer to him, Robin was receiving his tongue hungrily. She responded to the pressure of his thighs with pressure from hers. Her breasts gladly yielded to the exquisite pleasure of being pressed against him. She answered that kiss with her whole being, as though a repressive knot of caution inside her had finally come untied.

Jay took one hand from her bottom to cradle the back of her head, as if he knew she needed the support. Her mind was reeling, and all her senses were drowning. When he relinquished her mouth so she could speak, Robin gave a short soft gasp and whispered, "Jay . . . no, I don't know you! We're virtual strangers."

The hand that held her head closed around a thick rope of damp hair, then pulled back slightly—just enough so that her smooth and tender throat was exposed to the soft whisper of kisses with which he graced it. Then the tip of his tongue glided easily from the top of her neck to the small cleft in her chin. When his mouth found her ear, he whispered back, denying her protest. "I've known you for years and years, little lost Robin. You were never a secret here. I knew about you and idly wondered when you'd come here. Now that you have, I want you. Kiss me, Robin, kiss me now because you want me, too."

But she couldn't. His lips were making feather-soft strokes against her cheek, across the smooth hollow beneath the pronounced bone. He thrilled her all the more this way, and if she couldn't kiss him as he'd requested, she could press her body to his. Digging her fingers into his shoulders, she gasped audibly so he would know and revel in what he was doing to her.

Suddenly, he let her go and stepped back. Her entire body felt abandoned. She looked at him blankly, breathing shallowly through lips still parted by passion. Yearning wasn't recorded on his face. "What was that all about, Jay?" she demanded hoarsely. "Were you working the kinks out?"

"Shh, hush now. Keep your voice low, and smile."

Robin stared at him, flustered all the more by his bland, affable look. "Why did you say I should—"

"Caroline's about to come down the terrace steps," Jay interrupted. "Don't worry. You have a few seconds, and you look fine. Nothing shows. The best thing about a bathing suit is it can't get rumpled."

True, but everything not covered by the skimpy swimsuit must be blaring the truth. Now that she understood, she was grateful to him. "Thanks for the warning," she whispered, before plunging into the water and swimming to the deep end.

To Robin's surprise, Jay followed and swam alongside her to the far end of the pool and back. They stood up in the shallow end simultaneously, just as Caroline reached the wide pool deck.

"Isn't it glorious out here? I'm so glad we didn't have rain today, Robin! Well, have you two gotten to know each other?"

Robin merely smiled innocently back at Caroline. Caroline, whom she'd accused of being the blind and foolish toy of a young gigolo. *Ridiculous, just ridiculous*, she scoffed at herself.

3

ROBIN, JAY, AND CAROLINE were sitting on the terrace when the phone rang. The caller was a friend of Caroline's, and Robin had to endure the somewhat uncomfortable experience of overhearing herself being described to a stranger.

Jay listened, too, occasionally nodding his agreement, while Caroline grinned at Robin. When her friend finally got a chance to talk, Caroline covered the mouthpiece with her hand and whispered, "I can't help it. I'm so proud of you!"

Caroline went on and on about what a beauty Robin was—how she had natural fluffy waves of strawberry-blond hair that Caroline loved, how her cleft chin and gray eyes were just like Caroline's, how Caroline had truthfully never seen any woman as beautiful as Robin.

"I feel so blessed, Elaine. And I'm so lucky to have her here, because Robin's business is demanding and it isn't easy for her to get away. She's very, *very* successful, but with all her charm and intelligence that was assured."

"Tell Elaine about her ears and teeth. They're great. And her feet. She's got stunning feet." Though Jay was ostensibly speaking to Caroline, he was looking at Robin. His gaze slid over everything between her teeth and feet lingeringly, then returned to fasten on her eyes.

It was obvious even to Caroline that he was enjoying Robin's mild discomfort, and she leaned forward in her chair and gave him a pretend swat on the knee. *Be good!* her eyes warned maternally, causing him to chuckle.

"I'm going inside for a minute," Robin said softly to Caroline, not wanting to interrupt the phone conversation, but too embarrassed to hear more of it. She went to her room to comb her hair, and perhaps to cover anything that Jay might choose to admire. Anything, that was, except her ears, teeth and feet. Thinking of the way Eleanor wore her hair, pulled back in a severe bun, Robin decided to adopt the utilitarian style for the rest of this afternoon.

Fortunately Caroline was an exceptionally thoughtful hostess. On top of the marble vanity in the dressing room was a large round china tray with packets of hairpins, emery boards, cotton balls and other toiletries laid out for Robin's use.

She quickly pulled her hair back into a tight chignon. That done, she retrieved her white oval earrings from the dressing table, donned a white terry robe and slipped on white patent thongs. She had paused before putting the first earring on, wondering briefly why she was adorning herself with jewelry after settling on an unflattering hairdo.

"I love the earrings you're wearing," Caroline said a few minutes later. "I'm *never* without earrings, but mine are clip-ons. I wanted to have my ears pierced, because every now and then clip-ons bother me and if I take them off to give my ears a break I invariably lose one. But when I mentioned it to George he practically shuddered. I couldn't convince him that it was a convenience, not a mutilation. I could have it done now, of course, but I'd just feel guilty. So I go on having an occasional sore ear and losing earrings."

Robin shot Jay a superior look before responding to Caroline. "Mmm, well, fortunately nobody has had that sort of power over me."

"Caroline didn't ever have to bend her will to a man's power," Jay protested, "just his love, Robin. I'd say it's rather a misfortune for a woman to live without that sort of power in her life." Then, turning to Caroline, he said, "Speaking of earrings, why don't I ever see the diamond-and-emerald pair Dad gave you on your anniversary? I remember how excited he was about having them designed and made. And for good reason. They're a work of art."

"They are," Caroline agreed, her tone slightly wistful. To Robin she said, "The emeralds have crescents of diamonds around them, totaling the number of years George and I had been married." Then, softly, she added, "And that was the total. There were to be no more anniversaries."

Brightening as quickly as she had become melancholy, Caroline put her hand out to touch Robin's arm and said, "Robin, dear, I'd like you to have the earrings."

"Oh, I—I couldn't!"

"Please darling, don't refuse. It would thrill me to see them on you, and to know you would always have them." Caroline's voice was full of longing.

"Caroline, I don't know what to say."

"Say that you'll let me give them to you, and that I'll have the pleasure of seeing you wear them tonight!"

Turning to Jay before Robin could utter another word, Caroline said eagerly, "Jay, don't you think it's a good idea? And wouldn't your father have thought so, too? Help me convince Robin that she must take them."

A sardonic grin played on Jay's lips before he spoke. He lazily massaged his shoulder as he looked at Robin. It was the same shoulder that she had massaged with a passionately clinging hand.

"I don't think I need to say anything to convince Robin," he drawled. His fingers rubbed the hard burnished mass of his shoulder once more.

Caroline was oblivious to the nuances of the moment. "George would have thought it a wonderful idea. Once, on your birthday, I confessed to him that it hurt me every year that I couldn't give you a gift. Every year I fantasized about shopping for just the right thing. When I told George that, he said that I had given you the two best gifts in the world—life and your adoptive parents. And then he said to have faith, that the day would come when I'd be able to give you other gifts, as well. Well, now look, he was right. But then he always was. You will accept the earrings, won't you?"

If Robin could have spoken then, she would have said yes. She swallowed and licked her lips, but still she couldn't speak. She gave her answer to Caroline with a nod, a small smile and brimming eyes.

"I think this has been the nicest afternoon of—oh, I'd say the past ten years," Caroline mused a moment later, looking from Robin to Jay and then settling her contented gaze on Robin.

Robin could tell that Caroline was extremely pleased. It was as if by giving this one gift of great sentimental value, she had made up for all those birthdays when she hadn't been able to give her child anything. All the same, Robin was troubled by the great monetary value the earrings no doubt represented. But not as troubled as Jay, obviously.

Well, Jay could fret. Let him think she'd walk off with this house tucked into her tote, Robin decided. She would not let herself feel uncomfortable about his opinion of her again.

Like Jay, the patio furniture that George Lasalle had chosen to adorn his old brick terrace was getting to Robin. Despite her thick terry wrap, the metal of her chair was digging into her back. And although she managed a smile for Caroline's sake, she quite honestly would have placed most of this afternoon on a par with the day her car had been stolen. Two cartons of rare succulents ordered by her best client had been in the back.

Robin berated herself; Caroline deserved more than a half-hearted smile in return for her generous observation. "I think that meeting you has made this as nice as any afternoon of my whole life, Caroline," she offered, forgiving herself the white lie.

"I've enjoyed every minute of it, too," Jay enthused. "But incurable optimist that I am, I expect tonight to be even better."

"Well, it will be," Caroline assured him. "Because you'll be with us. It's just too bad that you don't have a change of clothes here, darling. I hate for you to have to drive home before we go out."

"No problem. I'm going to leave you ladies to enjoy the sun's finale without me. I'll have time to exercise Baxter that way, and I'll meet you at Canlis at nine." To Robin he explained, "Baxter's a Rottweiler. He loves to run on the beach."

"How nice," Robin said, omitting the phrase "that you're finally leaving." She wasn't interested in Baxter's exercise regime.

"Baxter is a gorgeous dog," Caroline asserted. "But I always feel that he suspects I'll walk off with something valuable when I leave. He's a born watchdog."

"Now, now, he doesn't even sniff your handbag."

Caroline chuckled. "He doesn't have to. He sniffs my hands for the odor of Steuben or Waterford." She explained to Robin that Jay collected art glass in his Kahala beachfront home.

"He has some pieces by Steuben that take my breath away. And I think Baxter knows where every piece belongs and makes a tour of the premises before he lets any guests leave."

"I think you should have a guard dog, Caroline," Jay said, turning the lighthearted conversation into something serious. "As a matter of fact, on your coming birthday I might surprise you with a Doberman."

"Don't you dare! You know I'm nervous about big dogs!"

"Me too," Robin added, sharing a smile with Caroline as they did every time they realized there was something else they had in common.

"But, Robin, surely you'll agree that Caroline's collection of art alone demands special security. And her jewelry is also irreplaceable. You just don't know, in this day and age, who might wander in on some innocent pretext and walk off with . . . with whatever."

Robin didn't need to see the gleam in Jay's eyes to know he was having fun with her. The *whatever* he'd referred to could only be translated into a pair of diamond-and-emerald earrings. She breathed deeply, widened her mouth into a sweet and insincere smile and otherwise ignored the subtle slur.

Caroline was begging Jay to drop the unfortunate topic of robberies and affirming her faith in her home's security system. "I paid a fortune for it, Jay. Surely it's reliable. And it doesn't shed on the carpet."

"I just have an insatiable desire to protect you," Jay said, leaning over to touch Caroline's hand. Then he stood up to leave.

Praise the Lord! Robin smiled, ready to say goodbye. He would be with them later, but even a brief reprieve from him and his innuendos would be appreciated.

"Jay, wait!" Caroline cried. "A letter for you, sent to this address, is on my dresser. I meant to give it to you earlier, but in my excitement I forgot all about it. It came yesterday. I'm sorry, dear."

"Don't be. It's probably a bill. You can give it to me later."

Give it to him later! Robin begged silently, but Caroline was already on her feet.

In another moment Robin was alone with Jay. They regarded each other. He smiled blandly. She showed no expression at all. Nothing he said was going to unnerve her or make her angry, she vowed, shifting her position on the punishing chair.

"I don't know what to make of you, Robin," Jay admitted. "I honestly don't. The only things I know for sure are that you're an ace swimmer and that you felt good in my arms and on my knees."

Robin blushed furiously. She still couldn't believe what had happened in the water. It was just incomprehensible that she would be so easily seduced by a stranger's purely physical attractions. And yet there she had willingly been, half in the water and half out, but completely immersed in Jeremiah Lasalle's embrace.

And oh, wasn't he just loving reminding her of it! Maybe they could have it out and reach an understanding. For his part, he could agree not to mention the pool episode again, and to refrain from burdening her with any more of his company than was necessary to keep Caroline happy. She, on the other hand, would agree not walk off with the butter knives or the crystal. But there was no time for such an exchange; Caroline wouldn't take much longer in getting back to them.

"Aren't we speaking to each other, Robin? You seem awfully quiet."

"What is there to say when one has just been completely humiliated. Should I gush, 'Thanks, Jay, I really needed to be brought down a peg or two.'" A smoldering emotional mix rose within her as she spoke, and the words were cotton in her dry mouth. She couldn't deflect the helpless feeling of vulnerability, and that bothered her enough to make her wish she had never come to Hawaii, despite her instant love for and rapport with Caroline.

Jay had effectively stolen the joy from the reunion, prejudging her as a fortune hunter. He thought her a pirate after the treasure of his own inheritance. And now, before the first day of her visit was out, she was wealthier by a pair of priceless earrings. Earrings that would more appropriately be given to Jay's wife when he married.

These thoughts welled up in her until she blurted out, "I didn't want the earrings, Jay! But how do you turn away a gift that comes from someone's heart? I really don't know how to do that. I owed it to Caroline to accept her gift. But I owe you no expla—" Robin suddenly realized how ludicrous her position was. She was sitting here flashing daggers at this man, insisting she owed him no explanation of her actions, and she had just finished passionately defending herself.

Surprisingly, Jay didn't grin or appear in any way to enjoy her self-imposed awkwardness. Frowning, he said, "You're right. I'm being repugnant, even to myself. Actually, I mentioned the earrings to Caroline in the hope that she would give them to you. I knew she didn't wear them anymore and that it would make her happy to see them on you. I'm delighted that you're going to have them."

Robin remained stubbornly silent.

Ignoring her obvious sullenness, Jay said nonchalantly, "This is a beautiful home, isn't it? But it's too big. Do you suppose Caroline has gotten lost?"

The inarguable thought popped into Robin's head that Caroline had lost her herself long ago in Jay's father. Her lack of independence was why she was rattling around in this house. And she could hardly decide anything for herself.

However, having already had her say, Robin decided to let things rest, especially as Jay was trying to be pleasant. "Perhaps Caroline stopped to talk with Mailia."

"Perhaps. Did you get a chance to look at the art? The Impressionist pieces are Caroline's pride and joy."

"Oh, I did. I couldn't get over the Renoir in the dining room, and the Monet in the guest bedroom is breathtaking."

Let him wonder if she would wind up being given or inheriting the Monet. She wouldn't deprive him of his angst. But it was odd to think of being Caroline's heir—if Caroline chose her to be. Being in this new situation really wasn't a problem for her, but it might be troubling for Jay. Maybe that was for the best, though. A problem of that magnitude might keep his mind off wanting to seduce her.

"How about the Dali? It's one of his most playful, from what I've seen of his work. And aren't the three Bonnards arresting? I would have to say they're my favorites, with the Monet a close runner-up."

Jay's tone was noncommittal as he offered these judgments. Anyone overhearing him would think he was engaging in casual conversation with someone who shared his appreciation of art. Robin knew otherwise. For all his having said he repulsed even himself with his behavior toward her, and that they should find the path to harmony, she knew he distrusted her.

Still, determined to keep her tone as light as his, she said, "Those too. The Bonnards are wonderful, and the Dali is certainly playful. I don't think I could choose a favorite in Caroline's collection. I'm spellbound by all that I see."

Robin shook her head violently, as if having to bottle up what she really wanted to say was creating a storm of rage in her mind. All she wanted was some information about herself and the friendship of her birth mother, and this wretched man with his suspicious mind made her furious.

When no hair swirled around her shoulders, Robin remembered the chignon. For a moment she'd forgotten her ploy to divert Jay's attention from her appearance. No need to have worried on that score, she thought angrily. She didn't give a hoot what he thought of her looks anymore. But what he thought of her character enraged her. "Shouldn't you be getting home to walk Baxter?" she asked pointedly. "I would gladly tell Caroline that you'll get the letter later tonight—if you're still planning on having dinner with us, that is." Her voice held a note of hope.

"I wouldn't dream of missing dinner, and Baxter can wait. He'll appreciate his reward all the more for having wondered if and when it would come."

Everything he said seemed to have a dual meaning, but Robin had decided not to play his game. She merely shrugged.

Jay leaned forward then, examining her. "You know, you do look very much like Caroline did when she was your age. And I can't blame her for gushing about you to her friends."

"Thanks," she said mechanically, brushing off the compliment. "It is fun to see how much Caroline and I have in common. Now that I've seen her collection, I think my love of art must have come from nature rather than nurture, too. My folks always collected books and loved music, but Caroline has made art an integral part of her life. I don't have anything like her masterpieces, of course, but I do buy good original art when I can."

Jay listened to this with keen interest. When she was finished he informed Robin that the Renoir, the Dali, the Bonnards and the Monet had all been purchased by his father.

To Robin, that comment was sufficient to close the subject of artistic appreciation as a genetic trait.

Jay apparently didn't think so. He asked if she had noticed *The Publican* by Eden in the upstairs study. It was, he said, his father's last purchase.

"I didn't, but I'll be sure to have a look at it." Then, compelled to get in one last word, she added, "Maybe I got my love of art from my father. My birth father, that is. If I ever meet him, I'll have to ask."

Jay's response to her comment was baffling. He quickly looked away from her to scan the horizon. It was obvious that the mention of her birth father had made him very uncomfortable.

When he finally looked back at her, Jay's expression was impassive. "You'll have to tell me all about the nursery business at dinner." The abrupt manner in which he spoke made Robin wonder what unpleasant thought he was covering up. "Horticulture is unknown territory to me. I only know a little about the plants common to the island," he continued in a more relaxed way.

"Then you wouldn't be interested in hearing about it." Robin realized she was being inexcusably rude, but by now she was completely unnerved, wishing Caroline would return.

"You're wrong. Ignorance doesn't preclude interest, Robin. Try to lighten up; we can have a good time together while you're here."

"You don't encourage lightening up!" A dull headache was beginning to throb in her temples, so she lifted her arms to gently massage them with her fingertips.

The direction of Jay's gaze informed her instantly that her movement had pulled the terry-cloth robe tight against her breasts. Her reaction was to think let him look, and let him remember the watery tryst, if he cared to. A memory was all he was ever going to have.

Jay suddenly leaned forward, startling her out of her reverie. "Oh, but I do encourage you to lighten up, in my way," he said, tracing the line of her jaw with one finger. He brought the fingertip to rest momentarily at the small cleft in her chin.

Robin sat as still as stone. Her arms were still raised, her fingers pressed to her temples. Hoping he hadn't noticed how his nearness was affecting her physically, she locked her unblinking gaze with his, willing him not to look down.

He was making soft circular motions against her chin with his index finger.

"Take your paw off my face or I'll hint to Caroline that I'd love to have a Renoir in my breakfast nook."

Jay grinned and nodded. "You do that, and Caroline will have that painting packed before you say 'nook' and then be begging you to take the Monet for the opposite wall." As he spoke, he moved the trespassing finger beneath her chin and trailed it lightly over her neck.

"The opposite wall has a window," she uttered absently, but whatever she would have said next was thwarted by shock. He placed his hand flat at the base of her throat, his thumb and index finger spread wide, encircling the graceful column like a necklace.

Very slowly and quietly, he said, "Caroline has a four-strand necklace of rubies and pearls with a diamond clasp. How beautiful the shortest strand would look resting here. . . ."

His hand stayed put, but his eyes roved to indicate where the longest strand would lie. His gaze returned to hers. "It would be especially beautiful when you wore your hair this way, so simple and elegant."

Robin could bear his touch and scrutiny no longer. She swallowed hard. The movement in her throat seemed like an intimacy against his hand. "Please don't do that," she commanded icily.

For a moment he didn't move. His eyes burned into hers with seeming arrogance, as though to say he knew she was hiding behind her cool facade, and he would do exactly what he chose to do. But he complied.

Robin sucked in the deep breath she so desperately needed. "I don't want you to touch me again, Jay."

"You sure? Touch is very important in any relationship."

"We have no relationship."

"No? Must be a lack of communication," he mused. "We should talk more. That's it. Let's see, plants could be our topic. Now tell me: Why succulents? That's your specialty, isn't it?"

He sat back and folded his arms across his chest, intent upon her reply, as if the history of Eagle Garden was really all he wanted to know.

"Yes, just succulents. We don't grow or sell anything else." She supposed she could set his mind at ease somewhat by informing him that Eagle Garden housed one of the world's largest collections of succulent plants. It was easily the best known nursery in Nevada, and it shipped orders all over America—including Hawaii. But of course she wouldn't brag to Jay of this; next to the Lasalle fortune her plant business, no matter how sturdy, would seem insignificant.

"And your reason for limiting yourself as you do?" he asked. "Wouldn't it be wise to . . . branch out? No pun intended."

Robin smiled. It was nice to hear him say something that didn't have seductive undertones. "I guess my mother and I stay with succulents because they're adaptors and survivors, as we are."

Jay cocked his head. He smiled slowly, though he appeared to be restraining a chuckle.

Robin, embarrassed and feeling a blush suffuse her face, couldn't blame him for finding her amusing. How pretentious she must have sounded, calling herself an adaptor and survivor.

"Good traits, those. It would be interesting to see a desert cactus transplanted to Oahu. I wonder if it would thrive in the lush environment. It's very steamy here, you know, especially compared to the thin dry atmosphere of Nevada."

Back to the double entendres, Robin observed. "It would depend on the succulent," she replied cautiously. "And on the capability of the person caring for it."

The look on Jay's face said clearly that she was the species of succulent he had had in mind. Whether he entertained the thought of her being transplanted here with hope or with fear, she couldn't tell.

"I live right on the beach," Jay informed her, another half-restrained chuckle evident. "If I decide to import a succulent, it'll have all the sand it needs."

Robin didn't respond, and made sure her gaze was innocent and ignorant. She hadn't grown up being called Robin Eagle without learning how to thwart exhaustive teasing by ignoring the first baiting remarks.

"Do you do much in the way of business and industrial landscaping?" Jay asked, rewarding her poise with a welcome change of subject.

"No, nothing like that. It's a relatively small business. We stay alive." She could imagine Eleanor rolling her eyes and then protesting this lie. But keeping Jay nervous about her being here was worth a little prevarication.

Just then the French doors opened and Robin turned her head to see Caroline approaching, letter in hand. Watching her, Robin realized once more what a refined and attractive woman her birth mother was.

As did many adoptees, Robin had experienced her share of nagging questions about who she was, whom she resembled, what she would look like as she grew older. Now that wondering was over. And Robin couldn't have wished anything better for herself than to age as gracefully as Caroline.

"Here I am! Did you think I got lost?" Caroline called gaily. "Mailia needed me in the kitchen. And I was wrong about having put the letter on my dresser. It was on my desk, in the sitting room. But before I thought to look for it there, I went to the garage and checked in the car. I get more absentminded every day, I'm afraid."

Caroline held an envelope out to Jay, and as he took it he said, "You have every right to be a little absentminded on as momentous a day as this."

Robin smiled and Caroline laughed, but Jay, having looked at what Caroline handed him, did not join in. He frowned, his amber eyes on the envelope. Almost imperceptibly, a muscle tightened at the back of his jaw, but Robin noticed.

The instantaneous change in his emotions was as noticeable as his strange reaction when she'd mentioned her birth father earlier. He looked hard at the envelope once more, and his chest rose on a sharp, audible breath.

"I'll see you ladies at nine," he said. He rose and bent to kiss Caroline's cheek lightly. Ignoring Robin except to give her a curt nod, he left.

4

"HE'S SUCH A DEAR," Caroline said fondly. "Ever since George died, Jay's been so wonderfully understanding. He knows that an affectionate kiss and a hug go a long way toward easing my loneliness. You see, for years and years his father spoiled me with constant affection. He knows it's been difficult... As a stepmother, I've been very fortunate—blessed, really."

Robin couldn't say anything. Caroline's having so little physical affection saddened her. Eleanor certainly didn't get more than an occasional peck on the cheek and a hug, but she didn't seem to need more to know she was loved.

Robin reflected that if a woman's self-worth had always been anchored to a man's love, and then the anchor wasn't there anymore, the woman was set adrift emotionally. She hoped the look in her eyes conveyed to Caroline that she understood.

"I'll tell you what I'm really going to treasure," Caroline said, brightening. "The three of us having our first dinner together. I just hope we run into someone I know, so I can have the thrill of introducing my daughter Robin, from Nevada. Of course, if that happens, you and Jay will have to hold me down or I'll float up to the ceiling."

"I promise to hold on to you real tight, and if by some slim chance we run into someone *I* know, I'll get just as big a thrill out of introducing you as my mother." Robin smiled, vowing that the animosity she felt toward Jay would not burst Caroline's balloon of happiness tonight.

She was wary of the evening, though. Serenity would not be on the menu, no matter what else was. Jay, of course, would look at her wearing Caroline's diamond-and-emerald earrings and imagine her with talons, beak and tail, looking for all the world like a vulture.

"Robin, there's something I feel I must say. I hate to make you feel uncomfortable, but I think it's better to get it off my chest and have done with it."

"You don't have to explain why you gave me up for adoption, if you don't want to," Robin put in quickly, anticipating what Caroline was struggling with. She wasn't overly worried about whatever she was going to hear, but, if the subject was distressing to Caroline, she wished they didn't have to go into it.

Caroline looked surprised. "Oh, no, it isn't that! Robin, I assumed you *knew* why I gave you up for adoption. It was because I was young, immature, unmarried, scared...and because I wanted a much better life for you than I had to offer. I wanted you to have a real family, a place in society that didn't cause you to cast your eyes down in shame, and I wanted you raised by a man and woman who had already done their growing up. I hadn't. I was still a child, my darling, and children shouldn't be raised by other children. Oh, Robin, I didn't *want* to, but I had to. And now...now I feel I'm overstating my case!" Caroline smiled gently.

Robin smiled in return, relieved and utterly at peace with Caroline's words. It was all so simple, so logical and so loving. "Caroline, I think you stated your case beautifully. When you gave me up, you did the right thing—the best thing. I really do believe that. Now tell me what was really bothering you, and don't worry about it making me uncomfortable. I'm sure it won't be anything I can't handle."

"My goodness...I'd almost forgotten what it was. Well, here goes, before I get cold feet...." Caroline took a deep breath and took in Robin's reassuring smile before she continued. "Robin, do you remember what Jay said about how unfortunate it is for a person to live without experiencing the sort of love George and I shared? Well, I couldn't help but feel it's tragic that neither you nor Jay have married. You're both such wonderful people. You should be tremendously loved, every day of your lives. Yet you're both alone."

Caroline sighed, then went on. "In Jay's case, I have to wonder if some parental failing on George's and my part has kept him from marrying again. Perhaps we were so happy together, so perfectly matched, that he's looking for perfection in a relationship. And in your case, I wonder if . . . well, perhaps being an adoptee affected your feelings about marriage."

"I . . . I don't know what to say. Except that I've never had any regrets about being alone. My adoption certainly doesn't have anything to do with my choice to remain single. Caroline, I . . ."

Robin floundered. She wanted to dispel Caroline's concern for her and really didn't know how to do it. Momentarily she considered telling Caroline about Marc and Keith, about how strongly she'd believed she would marry one, and how close she'd come to marrying the other. But she decided against it. Maybe some other time, but not now. It was all ancient history, anyway.

"Oh, darling, I'm sorry. . . .I don't know what got into me. I'm not usually one to pry. Heavens, I have dear old friends whom I wouldn't be so presumptuous with."

"It's all right, Caroline," Robin said to soothe the distraught woman. "It's more than all right. You're dear to be concerned, to care. But don't worry about me, please. I'm happy and living the life I want to live. I really love my work. I can't tell you how proud Eleanor and I are of Eagle Garden. I have lots of friends. If I lack anything, it's enough time to get involved in all the things that interest me. I don't cry into my pillow at night because I don't have a man. And I *don't* think marriage is the only path to fulfillment."

"You're right. It isn't. But it was in my generation, and some of the baggage we carry out of our youth stays with us, no matter how tattered and old-fashioned it becomes. I won't give it another thought. As of this moment the subject is permanently dropped—with regard to Jay, also."

At this mention of Jay, Robin realized she wanted to know much more about him, more than she had any business knowing. She knew why *she* was living her life alone; why Jay was doing so was an intriguing question.

She thought he was probably divorced—a young marriage had fizzled. Just maybe the example Caroline and George had set did have something to do with Jay's relationship with women, but Robin was willing to bet it wasn't a marriage of perfectly suited equals that he was looking for. He'd seen lots of love and open affection, granted, but he'd also seen an intelligent and loving woman who was willing to be subservient in marriage. He had probably expected the same behavior from a liberated wife and got a rude awakening.

"Is Jay divorced?" she asked.

"Oh, yes, for many years. His wife was one of those cheerleader types—peppy as a beach ball, with just about as much substance. But Jay adored Marcie. He was like a worshipful puppy around her. If Marcie had had her chest X-rayed, her heart would have showed up in the shape of a dollar sign, though. She married Lasalle Engineering, not Jay. George saw that quite clearly before Jay married, but he wouldn't say anything."

"He wouldn't? Why? I should think he'd want to warn his son."

Robin keenly remembered Eleanor's parental warnings—first about Marc, years later about Keith. The warnings had done no good, however. She'd gotten herself burned. Roasted.

"George might have wanted to step in, but he knew Jay wouldn't have listened. Just as I didn't listen to my mother . . . before you were born, Robin. So Jay was taken to the cleaners. He survived his ordeal and learned from it; he won't be easily taken again."

Nor would he trust easily again, either, Robin concluded.

"I'm glad *I* didn't listen to parental advice regarding love, Robin, or I wouldn't have had you. What a horrible, horrible thought!"

Robin threw her head back and laughed. "Oh, yes!" she agreed. "That would have been unfortunate for me. Thank you for your rebellious youth, Caroline! Thank you very much!"

Caroline chuckled and shook her head. "I'm going to have to confide something else to you, Robin, and I hope you'll take it as a sincere compliment. You don't just look like me. You look like your father, also, and he was a very handsome man. You carry many hints of him, even in your bearing. And you have his way of laughing. I remember the sound to this day."

Robin went from laughter to seriousness in a second. She had her father's laugh, and the knowing was important.

"Did he know about me?" she asked softly. She was overwhelmed by the need to hear that, yes, he had.

Caroline nodded. "He knew. He said he would marry me, but, Robin, he was young and scared to death of being a husband, much less a father, having to do all his growing up before he was ready. Don't resent him, dear, please. I don't."

"I don't..." Robin mused. "I...I've just tried not to think about him. I would fantasize about you all the time, never him. Maybe that was resentment. But I don't feel that way about him now, and—" She stopped herself. The idea of finding her birth father was rapidly gaining importance to her, and she wasn't sure yet whether to pursue it. Whether she was ready for it.

"And what?" Caroline prodded gently.

"I want to meet him," Robin said simply. "Do you think he'd mind?"

Caroline was beaming. "Oh, Robin. Meeting you will be the culmination of a dream for him, as it's been for me."

Robin was a bit awed by what she'd just decided to do, feeling eager, courageous and not just a little frightened. The emotional mix made her shiver and she broke out in goose bumps.

"Well, then, I'll do it!" she said firmly, rubbing her upper arms with slightly shaking hands.

"Wonderful! Oh, that's more than I ever hoped for, Robin. Shall we tell Jay tonight? We don't have to keep it a secret, do we?"

Robin assured Caroline that they needn't keep anything from Jay. A little sadly, a little angrily, she predicted that Jay would simply assume she was following up on another possible mark. She sighed. The mood was broken, the shivers gone.

JAY SAT IN HIS CAR in Caroline's driveway for a few moments. He held the large envelope, turning it over and over in his hands. He had to credit the investigator with being discreet. The postmark read Los Angeles, rather than Las Vegas, and it had been mailed to Caroline's address just as he'd instructed. Very few people knew details of Jay's personal life, including his home address and phone number. He preferred to keep it that way.

He told himself to open the letter. Whatever information it contained couldn't be any worse than what he'd already learned over the phone. Still, he hesitated. Robin was such a fantastic woman— nothing like the fortune hunter he'd anticipated. Intelligent, quick witted and hard working, she appealed to him in a way few, if any, women ever had. It was almost impossible for him to see her in the conniving role he had cast for her. Then, as if throwing cold water on himself, Jay thought of Marcie.

The Marcies of the world were legion, he reminded himself. As long as you had a certain amount of money and the power derived from having the respect of your peers, those women came out of the woodwork. He knew from experience.

After Marcie, there had been Lana. She had struggled valiantly to become the second Mrs. Jeremiah Lasalle, and might have succeeded. A bottle of champagne had been her undoing. It oiled her tongue sufficiently for her to gloat about Mrs. Jeremiah Lasalle being a bankable name.

There had been others. Many others. All different, yet all the same. It could make a man think seriously about becoming a monk.

He was acutely aware that people might want to prey on Caroline, too. He tried to protect her and prevent her from being taken advantage of, without being patronizing toward her. She was a capable person, active in the management of all her business affairs. But she was naive where people were concerned. She might set herself up to be hurt—both in the pocketbook and in the heart. While Caroline's devoted memory of her husband protected her from entanglements with men, a daughter was quite another matter. A stranger with a blood tie, a winning way and a real need for money might be in a position to break Caroline's heart.

Without further hesitation, he opened the envelope and scanned its contents—a letter and photograph. Stuffing both back into the envelope, he put them in the glove compartment, then started the car's engine.

Jay attempted to remain calm and reasonable. Sure the news was disappointing, but nothing he hadn't expected. He'd hoped, but he'd known better than to count on anything.

As the car cruised toward Kahala, he recalled the phone conversation he'd had with the private detective after the preliminary investigation. He had been told that Robin didn't see anyone steadily. She had been involved with a man by the name of Keith Floyd, but that had supposedly ended long ago. But there was one further detail: Keith Floyd was a compulsive gambler, in debt for more than a million dollars.

Jay had told the investigator to make sure there was no longer any connection between Robin and Keith Floyd. He wanted to know if she ever saw the man, even for fifteen minutes over coffee. He was about to end the conversation when the man brought him up short, saying, "Oh, yeah, about the natural father. He's dead. Ten years ago in a light plane. Nothing interesting on him. Bachelor. Civic-minded type with a small business in Cheyenne. Well respected. Minimal estate divided between a brother and sister."

Hanging up the phone, Jay had been thoroughly disgusted with himself. The nastiness of having someone investigated really hits home when all you find is that the person was just a nice guy...and that he had died tragically.

He'd felt even worse when Robin had said that if she met her father someday she would ask if he loved art. It had been hell sitting across from her and having that kind of information, especially when you had no business having it.

He had wanted to tell her—desperately. He'd wanted to tell her because she had a right to know that about her father, for God's sake. He had ached to put his arms around her and press her lovely head gently against his shoulder, so that if she needed to weep for the father she'd never met, he could comfort her. Instead he had turned away from her.

Having read this letter and seen the snapshot, Jay knew he should be feeling vindicated. But he wasn't; he was feeling worse than ever.

In his mind's eye he saw the photograph, neatly captioned: "The subject dining with Keith Floyd." It was dated just two weeks ago.

Jay pulled into his driveway, objectively regarding the graceful lines of his home. Kaname Tanizaki, his good friend and a talented architect, took justifiable pride in his achievements here. This house had all the essentials, all the luxuries, all the conveniences belied by its graceful simplicity. It just didn't have any human warmth, and sometimes Jay longed for someone to share all that he had.

Well, at least there was old Bax to come home to. He greeted the dog affectionately. There was no sense in spoiling Baxter's wriggling happiness just because Robin Eagle had not broken off with Keith Floyd. What was it to Bax that Robin had probably promised to bail good friend Keith out of his million-dollar debt after this trip?

"She's got a pair of earrings worth a lot of bucks, but she's got a long way to go if she's aiming for a million," he mused aloud to himself.

Baxter whimpered and did a little dance to remind Jay that it was time for a beach run. "Sorry, Bax. Tomorrow," he muttered, sinking into a chair.

He hoped Robin wouldn't sell Caroline's earrings. She couldn't get anywhere near their worth if she did. Besides, they shouldn't be sold. Not ever. Hell, if she was going to sell them, he'd buy them from her and give her a fair price.

Jay got up one minute after sitting down and went grumpily into the shower. Sluicing water washed away Robin Eagle's touch, but not the thought of her.

Dressed in a well-tailored gray suit, Jay was ready to go, but the clock on his nightstand told him there was time to kill. A Scotch and water wouldn't be unkind about now, he decided.

At the bar he poured himself a drink, then sat back to assess the situation. A woman had had her privacy grossly invaded, although she didn't know it. She also felt a fool because in her exhausted state she'd let a flurry of infatuation carry her away. But she was no more foolish than he; he'd felt the attraction, too. And his crude behavior in the pool was inexcusable under any circumstances.

That wasn't all, though. No, the woman had also been subjected to less than subtle character assassination. He had done all this to her simply because she had somehow hooked up with a loser. It wasn't fair. In fact, it was rotten.

Jay leaned down and rested his brow on Baxter's for a moment. The dog had been sitting erect and intent by the bar, much like a good buddy waiting to hear the punch line in a story. It was a peaceful communication man and dog shared from time to time. Jay was certain it did them both a world of good.

Leaving his untouched drink on the bar, Jay got up, locked the house and took fast strides to his car. He would buy Robin a gift, he planned, a peace token. Not that he could apologize adequately for the wrong he had done her—not yet, anyway.

"YOU LOOK BEAUTIFUL!" Caroline told Robin appreciatively.

"Why, thank you," Robin said happily. "And may I say *you* look stunning."

While getting ready to go out, Robin had had
conflicting desires. She didn't want Jay to think she
was dressing up for his benefit, yet she wanted to
look her best for Caroline. Smiling at the slightly
embarrassing but sweet memory of Caroline's afternoon telephone conversation, Robin had slipped
into her favorite dress.

Feathered waves of strawberry-blond framed her
face and throat when her makeup was complete. In
styling her hair she had made sure that it would not
hide the exquisite earrings she was wearing.

Caroline stood back to admire Robin once more
and commented, "I was just wondering, darling, if
that dress isn't begging for a necklace." She paused.
"What do you think?"

Robin pursed her lips and looked down at the
white linen against her chest, considering it. She
didn't like to go heavy on the jewels, and besides the
earrings, she was wearing a slender white-gold ser-
pentine watch and a dainty ring that had belonged
to Grandma Edith, Eleanor's mother.

But Caroline was right. This simple and modest
neckline probably needed some enhancement. She
nodded and said, "It does look bare. I have a pen-
dant I can wear with it."

"Wait right there!" Caroline cried. She turned
and was instantly out of the room. Robin waited,
holding her breath and hoping Caroline wasn't

going to return with the necklace Jay had mentioned, praying she would be carrying something understated, inexpensive and of no interest to Jay.

She need not have worried about the ruby necklace. A beaming Caroline came back to the living room with a breathtaking piece, but not with *the* necklace.

Robin told Caroline forcefully that she would be glad to *borrow* the jewelry to wear on this trip—but that was all.

"Nonsense! It's yours forever! Wear it in good health and you'll be making me happier than you can know."

Caroline secured the clasp for Robin. Now a single strand of the purest pieces of jade adorned and highlighted Robin's bodice.

"George and I bought it in Hong Kong, on a trip we took one Christmas. Jay might remember it. He was with us."

"Caroline . . . really, I wish you wouldn't. . . ."

"Hush. No more of that. This is just what George would want me to do. Now, shall we go? Jay will worry if we're late, and we don't want that."

No, we certainly don't, Robin thought grimly.

5

CANLIS DELIGHTED ROBIN. The subtle Polynesian decor was complete with lava rock, a waterfall behind the piano bar and an entire wall lavishly decorated with orchids. On entering the venerable Waikiki establishment, she quickly realized that this was where the local people came to be pampered while enjoying superb cuisine. If there were other tourists here besides herself, they weren't obvious.

Dinner, served by a quietly efficient kimono-clad Polynesian waitress, had wound to a satisfying end. Robin had thoroughly enjoyed her seafood, broiled over kiawe wood, and knew she would recall the delicate taste every time she ordered the same dishes in less worthy restaurants and wound up with something mildly disappointing. The evening's memory she would most treasure, though, was of the happiness she and Caroline had shared.

Robin smiled when Caroline, putting her coffee cup on its saucer, verbalized that same feeling. Looking at her radiant mother, then, Robin felt very close to her. The evening had been much more relaxed than she'd anticipated before they had met Jay. She had expected him to make some remark— subtly camouflaged but accusatory nonetheless— about the precious jewels she was wearing.

He had not. If he'd been surprised when she walked into the restaurant wearing Caroline's exquisite necklace, as well as the stunning earrings his father had designed, he didn't show it. His eyes had traveled over Robin appraisingly as he smiled a warm greeting, but they had not rested for even a second on any gem.

"You look much too radiant for a woman who's traveled so far in one day," he had told her, the look in his eyes underscoring his sincerity. "And you look ravishing, as always," he had said to Caroline, kissing her affectionately on the cheek.

"Thank you, dear. My goodness, what is that? What a strange centerpiece." Caroline had scanned the tables nearby before adding, "None of the other tables have potted plants on them."

"It doesn't belong to the restaurant," Jay had explained. "I bought it for Robin, so she would feel at home."

Robin and Caroline had both looked from the furry panda plant to Jay, and back again to the plant. Then they burst out laughing. Robin had hurried to comment that the fuzzy-leafed brown-speckled plant was one of her favorites. "I love it," she said. "And I have the perfect place for it, in my breakfast nook." The truce had been in effect from that moment onward.

Jay had smiled then, and explained, "I wanted Robin to have at least one succulent to look at while she's here, and this one appealed to me because of the clay dove, symbolizing peace."

Robin had concluded from Jay's words and smile that he had been remembering the afternoon sparring, and that he was glad to have the animosity over with.

She smiled at Jay now, grateful for the serenity he had helped bring to the evening. If he hadn't wanted this dinner to be pleasant for her, it wouldn't have been. But he'd been a prince since she and Caroline had arrived at Canlis. All through dinner they'd enjoyed conversation without double entendres, hints of suspicion or artfully concealed sarcasm.

That had set the mood for an entire evening of gaiety. Robin noticed that the only time Jay seemed at all troubled was when, at Caroline's urging, she'd confided to him that she was going to seek her birth father. Jay seemed at a loss for anything to say about that. Without even a pretense of subtlety, he'd steered the subject to the sights of Oahu that he intended to show Robin.

Leaning back in her chair, Caroline sighed and said, "I'm afraid my age is showing. I think I should go on back to Diamond Head alone and leave you two to finish the evening. I certainly don't want you to cut the night short because of me. Jay, why don't you—"

Jay jumped in before Caroline could finish. "I'm going to take the words right out of your mouth," he said, then invited Robin to go for a drive.

Robin knew what was coming next and prepared to convincingly echo Caroline's plea of exhaustion. In truth she wasn't tired at all, which was odd, considering the length and events of the day. Even the champagne she'd had with dinner should have made her sleepy, she thought, but it hadn't. Still, she'd rather forgo a late night drive through Honolulu with Jay. He was even more dangerous to her now that he liked her and had brought forth the dove of peace. She had felt more secure when he suspected her of coming to Hawaii with larcenous intentions.

She thanked him for suggesting the tour, but declined, saying she was feeling the effects of the long day. A little disappointed at her own words, but knowing that she had made the right decision, she lifted her coffee cup and took a sip.

"You'd probably be in bed sooner if you went with him, darling," Caroline said.

Robin managed to swallow her coffee without choking. Her cheeks flushed from the shock of Caroline's words, however, and she darted a glance at Jay to see if he was similarly appalled.

Jay looked absolutely innocent. He nodded thoughtfully and said, "That's true. You would be."

For a moment Robin thought that either she or they were mad, but then Jay explained. "If you go home in Caroline's car, she's not going to be able to resist sitting up for hours talking to you, Robin. As exhausted as she is, she won't be able to relinquish your company. If, on the other hand, you come for a short drive with me, Caroline will be asleep before you even get home, which means that you'll both get a decent night's rest. But it's up to you. If you'd rather stay up till dawn talking with Caroline, be adamant in rejecting my offer."

Unable to argue with that kind of reasoning, Robin gave in. "When you put it that way, I'd love to go for a drive." A chuckle of pure relief accompanied her capitulation. This was all perfectly innocent and she was merely being paranoid, she decided.

Or was it so innocent? Jay, she noted, now looked suspiciously well satisfied with events. He had begun stroking one of the panda plant's felt-like leaves. "Amazing how good this funny little succulent feels to the touch," he said, looking at Robin.

She returned the appraisal. His thick sun-bleached hair was the color of an antique coin in the room's dim light, and his eyes gleamed with a blend of humor, intelligence, health and power. The overall impression he gave was one of casual elegance.

"Shall we be off?" Jay suggested, signing the dinner check with a flourish and gathering up the plant.

The parking attendant brought Caroline's car first, and after Caroline waved and drove off, Jay put an arm around Robin's waist. He leaned down and murmured close to her ear, "Don't worry about a thing. The warty toad of this afternoon is gone forever."

They drove down Kalakaua, Waikiki's main thoroughfare. For Robin, the massive structures lining both sides of the brightly lit street were somewhat reminiscent of Las Vegas. In Waikiki's hotels, though, tourists were sleeping off the voluptuous pleasures sunny days on Oahu plied them with.

But in Las Vegas hotels, nighttime was not for sleeping. There the tourists stayed awake almost beyond human endurance, in order to have added hours for gambling.

"So many large hotels in one area make me think of home," Robin mused. After making the comparison, she added, "I confess that Waikiki is much lovelier, even with the excess of development."

"I'm going to confess something, too," Jay said. "I don't like Las Vegas at all."

"Because of gambling?" Robin asked, knowing that the answer would be yes. Some people loved to gamble and some were terribly uncomfortable with it. In Las Vegas, gambling went on day and night, but Robin was indifferent to that aspect of her hometown.

Though she never gambled so much as a dime away, other people's doing so didn't faze her. That she'd loved and almost married a man who gambled compulsively, so compulsively that his life had finally become a tragic shambles, hadn't even turned her hostile toward her town's main industry. Healthy people didn't behave as Keith did. They lost or won some money at the casinos and then quit. Robin could even see virtue in legalized gambling; it had brought people and prosperity to Nevada. In moderation and for the purpose of recreation, games of chance gave a lot of people pleasure.

"It is the gambling that bothers me most about the place, but not only that," Jay said. "I've been there twice, both times on business. And both times it seemed I saw thousands of people from all over desperately searching for fun and for the pot of gold at the end of the rainbow. They'd go from slot machines to shows to gaming tables and then start the cycle over again. It depressed me."

"Jay?"

He turned and looked at her.

"Isn't that why every day thousands of people from all over come here? Only instead of gambling and seeing exciting shows until they drop from exhaustion, they wear leis around their necks until the flowers die. They long for the romance of old Hawaii, but stay at big modern hotels that have nothing Hawaiian about them. They eat pseudo-Hawaiian food that they don't really like at expensive phony luaus, and sit in the sun on crowded beaches until they sunburn. And they're happy doing all these foolish things, just the way tourists in Las Vegas are happy gambling and seeing shows. And they make Hawaii prosperous. Am I right, or am I right?"

Jay looked at her, with the beginning of a smile playing on his lips, and then he turned his attention back to driving. "You're more than right," he admitted. "You're keenly perceptive for someone who hasn't been to a phony luau yet or sat on a crowded Waikiki beach getting sunburned." He shot her a quick teasing look.

"I knew I was right," she said, laughing. She leaned her head back on the headrest, feeling good about everything, even about having rallied to the defense of her hometown. To put the cap on this loyalty, she added, "Las Vegas has numerous attractions beyond the casinos. Next time you're there on business, I'll show you the town and give you a different perspective on it."

"I'll bet you could make me want to stay forever," he said softly. "Do you know where I'd like to take you now, while I'm showing my town off to you?"

"No." Robin smiled. "But I think you should take me back to Caroline's. You told her that this would be a short drive, and it hasn't been. She might worry about us. She's very maternal, and mothers do most of their worrying late at night."

Jay laughed and said that Caroline had done her share of late night worrying, especially when he got his first car. "But she won't worry tonight," he promised. "She's sound asleep already—I guarantee it. So I'll just take you to see Lasalle Engineering's headquarters in Ala Moana, and then we'll head back for Diamond Head. Is that all right?"

Robin wasn't sure that it was. Having her alone very late at night in a deserted office building where he was boss could make Jay want to engineer a little passion.

"Someone's there. We won't be alone," he assured her, as if having read her thoughts.

"Someone is? Do engineers work more efficiently at night?" she asked, then prayed he wouldn't take advantage of such a tempting straight line.

Jay wasn't laughing when he replied, "Some do. I know one that does, anyway. We're almost there. Our offices are on the eleventh story of the Ala Moana Building. I'll show you a great view after I introduce you to Dan Riley—an Irishman, a baseball nut and a workaholic. Dan's finishing up an important job this month but he always works crazy hours. He's really more productive at night, and then he'll sleep half the next day."

"Oh. Well, I'll enjoy both meeting Dan Riley and seeing the view from Ala Moana."

Jay just nodded.

When Jay said a cheery good evening to the security officer and signed into the building, Robin had a suspicion, despite Jay's promise, that this uniformed man was the only other person on the premises. Even the maintenance crew would have gone home by now, she thought. In the elevator she felt a little anxious, uncertain how much she trusted herself with Jay, but she wasn't at all angry. He'd wanted her up here where they would be alone, so he'd made up a story to get his way. If she really hadn't wanted to come she wouldn't have bought the story, she told herself.

"Elevators. They take forever," Jay commented.

Robin nodded affirmation.

The door to Lasalle Engineering was locked, though there were lights on inside. "It's me, Dan," Jay called, after unlocking the door and holding it open for Robin.

A man who was obviously engrossed in his work slowly responded. "Yeah, I'm back here, Jay."

"Thought I was faking about having an Irish night owl on the staff, didn't you, Robin?" Jay teased in a low voice.

A few minutes later, having walked with Jay past executive offices, many cubicles, and rows of empty tables in the vast drafting room, Robin was being introduced to a young-looking paraplegic. She was even more pleased about Jay's neglecting to mention Dan Riley's wheelchair-bound state than she was that he hadn't been lying about there being someone in the office.

After some friendly conversation with the structural engineer, Robin decided she liked him immensely; he had a delightful personality and a quick wit.

"Let's introduce Robin to the rest of the staff, Jay," Dan proposed, after which Robin found herself being escorted, with Dan in front and Jay behind her, from one empty table or desk to the next.

Lasalle Engineering took on an international flavor as Dan and Jay maneuvered her through the office, putting names to the empty places. "At least you don't expect me to shake hands with everyone," Robin said breathlessly as she was whisked by yet another desk. "And please don't expect me to remember all the last names!"

"Just first names, where everyone sits and what everyone's coffee mug looks like," Dan said.

When Robin had met everybody who wasn't there, including the receptionist who was leaving in a week and the Canadian woman who had been hired to replace her, Jay took her to his own office, leaving Dan Riley to his work.

"It's wonderful that Dan can be so independent, being here without anyone to give him assistance," Robin commented.

"I'm so used to his self-sufficiency that I don't think about it," Jay commented. He came and stood beside Robin by the window wall behind his huge teak desk. Putting a hand on her shoulder he said, "Look to your right. Way over there is the—"

"It's nice that you told me he was an Irishman and a workaholic, but not that he's paraplegic," she interrupted. "You didn't think that factor had much to do with him as a person, or was even very interesting."

"Uh huh. Way over to your right is—"

"My mother's in a wheelchair."

"Yes, I know. Can you see that cluster of lights—"

"Jay, how did you know?" Robin asked, turning to face him. When she did that, his hand that was resting lightly on her shoulder came around her arm and caressed her.

She stepped back, but not because the increased physical contact disturbed her. She really wanted to know how Jay had come by that information about Eleanor. Caroline hadn't known about it until early this evening, when they were alone together, talking on the terrace.

When she and Caroline phoned and wrote to each other, Robin never mentioned Eleanor's handicap because there wasn't any reason to, just as Jay had not said anything about Dan Riley's physical condition. Caroline hadn't been alone with Jay this evening; she wouldn't have had a chance to tell Jay that Eleanor Eagle was in a wheelchair, not without Robin's hearing her do so.

Robin was sure that *she* hadn't mentioned it to him in the course of the day.

Jay pretended to sigh. "I cannot get you interested in the view," he complained. "Being Las Vegas born and bred, are you so jaded by night lights
that you're not even intrigued by them?"

"No, certainly not, but I'm more interested in
how you knew about my mother. Did I tell you that
she was paralyzed?"

"No, Caroline did. She mentioned it a while ago,
when you two were corresponding."

Robin conceded to herself that she must have
mentioned it in a letter and forgotten that she did.
It was odd, though, that Caroline had also forgotten.

This evening, when Robin related the story of
Eleanor's accident and injury to Caroline, Caroline had looked stricken, commenting that Eleanor
had had more than her share of suffering.

"She's had her share of happiness, too," Robin
had assured Caroline with a smile, but she was
moved by her genuine concern.

Trying to pay attention to the distant lights that
Jay was pointing out to her, Robin reasoned that
she and Caroline had both been so excited about the
reunion and had so many facts about each other's
life to absorb that they'd probably forgotten a lot
of the information already exchanged.

She turned away from the window when Dan

Riley stopped outside the doorway to Jay's office. "I'm leaving," he announced. "These other guys can work till dawn if they want to, but I've got to get some sleep. See you tomorrow, Jay. Good meeting you, Robin. If I don't see you again, enjoy your stay on Oahu."

"You'll see Robin again," Jay promised him.

"He's nice," Robin told Jay when Dan had left. "And so is your office and the view from your office, and so is your entire staff. But it's time for us to be going, too."

Jay sat down on the edge of his desk, which wasn't the action of a man about to leave his office. "Why?" he inquired simply.

"Well, it's late, for one thing. I'm tired." It wasn't true, and a self-conscious grin followed the falsehood.

"Robin Eagle, you look as if you've just had eight hours of sleep."

"Mmm, well, try this one. You have a full day of work ahead of you tomorrow. I'm keeping you up." This was quite true, so she was able to look serious while saying it.

She hoped a third or fourth reason wouldn't have to be offered. If he didn't lift his fanny from the desk and begin to escort her out of the deserted office, though, she was eventually going to have to tell him the truth, and she didn't want to.

He shook his head. His hands had been on the desk's edge but now he folded his arms across his chest. Robin knew that this was not the motion of a man about to walk through a doorway.

"No good," Jay said. "I'm not going to work very much tomorrow. I'm going to spend most of the day with you. And I couldn't feel tired in your presence if I wanted to."

"Reason number three: you're neglecting Baxter." She smiled triumphantly.

"It's a dog's life," Jay said, smiling back and chuckling softly.

Robin sighed and clasped her hands in front of her chest. His behavior had been absolutely perfect all night, and she knew that he was only teasing now. If she became even slightly adamant, they would leave immediately.

Actually, she didn't want the evening to end. If there had been other people around, or if he had suggested going to a public place, she would have been happy to stay out later. But she was uncomfortable there. "But what about my virtue?," she offered with exaggerated coyness. "Why, the security guard and your entire staff will be wondering what we're doing up here."

He grinned, going along with her ploy. "Oh, the wickedness in people's minds! We'd better get out of here if we're going to protect your good name."

Jay stood up, and Robin found herself looking into seductive yet mirthful eyes. Before she had time to catch her breath, she was being propelled toward the door.

"We'll go right to my house, and nobody will wonder about anything," Jay said when the elevator doors closed.

"We certainly will not."

"Whatever you say," Jay murmured, turning her into his arms and brushing her lips with his. "We can stay right here."

Robin was about to protest when his lips, seeking warmth, came down over hers again, stilling her words. His taut, maddeningly desirable body molded against hers deliciously. His scent, the feel of him, his touch were so sweet that Robin was beyond speech when the elevator doors slid open on the ground floor.

6

DRIVING ON KEALAOLU AVENUE, they passed the grounds of the Waialae Country Club. Jay golfed there on the rare morning he had the time.

"You're seeing the world's longest hibiscus bush," he informed Robin.

On the longest day of my life, Robin thought in wonder. Whether it was the jet travel, the reunion with her birth mother, Hawaii's sensuous allure, the exotic restaurant, or—most likely—Jay's kisses, something had obviously robbed her of her reason.

Just then, Jay pulled the Rolls to a silent stop in front of a sprawling beach-front house. Taking the keys from the ignition, he commented, "The best things about living in Kahala are that it's tranquil, it's never humid and the beach is excellent for swimming and surfing. Believe it or not, I still get out there and surf."

"I can believe that, but I can't believe I'm sitting here in your driveway in the middle of the night."

"Why not?" Jay asked, leaning over to kiss her hair. Before she could answer, he took her chin in his hand and gently tilted her head back so she would have to look into his eyes. "I'll tell you something you *can* believe," he said. "I'm not going to touch you, Robin. I'm not going to take advantage of having you in my nest. I'll introduce you to Baxter, and then the three of us will walk on the beach. At this hour, it's a sublime experience. And if anyone gets out of line, it'll be Baxter, not me."

Looking into his warm eyes, feeling reassured as much by his character as by his promise, she responded, "Let's go inside, Jay. I'm dying to meet this animal."

They were greeted at the door by an excited Baxter. Robin extended her hand for him to sniff, while Jay informed him, "You may kiss Robin, Bax. I already squared it with her."

Baxter did just that, swiping the back of her hand with his enormous wet tongue. Then he beamed a dog grin at his master and wagged his tail vigorously.

"I think he's telling me to eat my heart out," Jay ventured.

Robin looked askance at her hand. "I think I'd better wash up," she said with a rueful grin, at which Jay pointed her in the direction of the guest powder room.

When she came out, he was dressed just as he'd been before except that he'd loosened his tie, taken off his shoes and socks and rolled his pants up above the ankle. Standing in the dimly lit sunken family room, he looked wonderful to Robin. He was half the meticulously attired professional man-about-town, half the little boy embarking on a beach romp with his dog. And she found him totally appealing.

"Still game for a walk?" he asked. "We can stay here, if you'd rather." He indicated a curving sectional sofa with a sweep of his arm.

"I'd love a walk," Robin said firmly. She glanced down at her feet. She decided she should leave her shoes in the house, as Jay was doing; walking on the beach in high heels would be terribly awkward.

"Better leave your shoes here," Jay suggested, as though reading her thoughts. "The heels would sink in the sand."

"Er, yes, but—" She looked down at her sheer white stockings.

"Panty hose? You're right, they'll get runs. Just go in there and take them off, then you can get back into them before I take you home." He offered the practical advice without changing his innocent expression. It was as though he had just suggested she leave her handbag in the house.

Once again she retired to the powder room and returned feeling somewhat naked under her cotton dress.

"Okay, Bax, the lady's ready," Jay informed him. "Lead the way."

"It's uncanny how that dog understands what you say," Robin marveled. On Jay's last word, Baxter had turned and headed for the sliding glass door to the rear deck.

They hadn't been on the beach for more than a minute when two small, sturdy boys ran laughing past them.

"Wait up!" Jay called. "Tim! Kevin! Why aren't you in bed? What are you doing outside so late? Have you been mining the beach again?"

The boys hopped in place rather than interrupt their seemingly perpetual motion. One said that they were being allowed to stay up extra late because their grandfather had arrived on the island that afternoon. "It's like a holiday! We don't want to go to bed! We get to stay up because we're too excited to sleep!"

Jay placed a large hand on each boy's nape gently, as if handling puppies, and turned them to face Robin. "These are the Kurosawa twins," he told her. "Tim and Kevin. They're neighbors, and very good neighbors, except that they like to play war and mine the beach with all sorts of contraptions. Once I stepped on a balloon they'd just barely buried in the sand. It nearly took ten years off my life."

"That was to stop the Martians from invading!" announced one of the boys, while the other corroborated his story. "Yes, Mr. Lasalle! That wasn't for you! That was for the invaders! It was there to protect you!"

"Well, we're the only invaders on the beach tonight, so be sure there aren't any surprises for us," Jay warned, letting go of the boys. "And then get on home. It's too late for you to be out." The boys ran and skipped toward their house, giggling conspiratorially.

"I'll bet they mined it," Jay said. "But we'll be careful."

They walked slowly, Jay with his hands jammed into his front pockets and Robin with her hands behind her back, her index fingers linked together.

"Kids don't change," Jay said. "Each of those boys has a personal computer, stereo and portable cassette player. They have a VCR. But give them a chance to stay up late and they'll spend the time doing something worthwhile—trapping Earth-invading Martians."

"Thank goodness," Robin murmured.

"Do you like kids?" Jay asked, looking at her.

"Sure. But I'm not around them often. Sometimes we have seventy or so little kids at the nursery at one time, on a field trip. But you don't get to know children that way, not the way you seem to know the twins."

"When I watch those kids at play I remember how much I wished for a brother when I was that age," Jay mused. "I hated being an only child. Did you?"

Robin thought about it, then stopped walking long enough to answer. "I didn't know if I really was an only child. Of course, environmentally I was. But it seemed improbable that neither of my birth parents wouldn't have had other children. Now that I know Caroline didn't, I'm a bit curious to find out if my father did. I guess it's one of the reasons I'm going to look him up."

Jay didn't answer, and they walked on in silence. There was enough light from a few scattered houses and the moon for them to make their way with ease. The sand was smooth and the air was so balmy crisp, so redolent of the clean scent of the sea that Robin's senses came alive as she walked. "I love it here," she murmured.

"Me too. I've never yet come out here at night without feeling blessed."

It was a simple but lovely thing to say, telling Robin a lot about Jay and his sensitivity. Unfortunately, the spell was broken when she suddenly lost her footing, wrenching her ankle painfully. She couldn't restrain a resounding "Ouch!"

Jay gripped her elbow, keeping her from falling to the sand. She'd stepped into a slimy water-filled hole at the bottom of which was a sharp object that caught her between her first two toes. The pain from her ankle vied with the rest of her foot for attention.

"Are you all right, Robin?" Jay asked quickly. "Here, put your arm around my shoulder. Let me look at your ankle."

"Ooooh, it isn't my ankle," Robin replied, wincing. "Not entirely! Something gave me a nasty jab!" She had to stop speaking for a moment and catch her breath.

"I'm going to give those boys a piece of my mind when I see them," Jay muttered angrily. "I've told them over and over that someone would be hurt someday."

Robin gratefully felt the pain subside, and she examined her big toe as Jay bent to inspect her ankle. "They didn't mean to snag a human. The trap was for Martians," she said. "I'm just glad Baxter didn't step in the hole and break his leg."

"Well, it isn't funny. You were hurt."

Jay was so cross that Robin impulsively caressed the shoulder her hand rested on, to assure him that it was all right. "It's not all that serious," she reassured him. She took her arm from his back, and though she gingerly held her toes off the sand, stood on both feet again.

Jay took off his lightweight jacket and laid it on the sand, lining side up. "Here, sit down and rest. I'll check your wounds," he said.

He helped her to sit down, then squatted on his heels in front of her. "Let me have that foot again. I really couldn't get a good look before."

Robin suddenly felt very shy about this attention. To place her bare foot in Jay's outstretched hands seemed too intimate. "Why don't you see what was inside the hole?" she quickly suggested. "I'd like to know what bit me."

He put a finger on her knee, lightly. "Don't you want me to examine your foot?"

"I . . . well . . ."

He took his finger from her knee. "Right. I'll see what bit you." Effortlessly he sprang to his feet. He went back to where Robin had tripped, stuck his hand down into the hole and fished out a plastic bag with a dozen or so broken shells in it. Four chopsticks buried in the sand had kept the bag from collapsing.

"I'm going to tell those boys once more that they're not to set traps on the beach, and if they don't take the warning to heart I'm going to speak to their dad," Jay vowed, holding the sophisticated weapon out for Robin to see. He tied the bag closed then, saying, "I'll keep this for evidence."

She laughed, looking up at him. "I'm relieved. It could have been a scorpion or something. But I guess there aren't any scorpions on Hawaiian beaches. The tourist bureau would be aghast at my imagining such a thing."

Jay hunkered down again and put the plastic bag behind him where Robin couldn't see it. "Robin, I lied to you. I didn't want you to be frightened," he said very seriously, his amber eyes fastened on hers. No television doctor with dour news to impart could have been any more convincing.

Robin chuckled, anticipating what he would say. She even murmured the words along with him. "It was a scorpion."

Jay nodded solemnly. "It sure was. I've got him in the bag. Dreadful looking, the biggest I've ever seen. You'd better let me examine that foot."

She did. He held it in his hands very gently, two fingers stroking the ankle, which no longer hurt at all. "Just as I thought," he intoned, having brushed the wet sand from wherever it clung to her foot. He gently tweaked her toe. "You have a condition that's often found on Hawaiian beaches, but I've never ever seen as advanced a case as yours."

"Oh, Jay!"

"Don't laugh, Robin. If you hadn't stumbled on the sophisticated weaponry of the Kurosawa boys, I might not have detected your condition tonight. No, I'm sure I wouldn't have. We have to thank fate that I did and that by using gentle massage I can save the entire foot."

He'd said all this while looking at the small shapely foot in his hands. Now he looked into her eyes. Robin shook her head, smiling gleefully. "Jeremiah Lasalle, you missed your calling," she informed him. "There's a TV series doctor in you, aching to come out. I can almost see the stethoscope dangling from your neck."

He nodded reflectively, again caressing her ankle. The thumb of his other hand moved slowly over her instep. "Possible. Possible," he murmured, continuing the massage. "We could call the series *Hawaii General*. You would play a patient who winds up in my care over and over again." As he spoke, Jay moved his hands to just above her ankle and gently massaged her calf.

She took in a deep breath, watching his long masculine fingers moving against her leg. "Jay. . ."

"In one episode, you'd be wan and frail and I'd tell your worried mother—Caroline would be excellent in the role because she's photogenic and worries easily—that she should go home and get some rest. I would promise her that I'd stay in your room all night long, applying healing massage even as you slept."

He'd reached a hand to her shoulder moments ago; now it glided down her arm. She shivered, again imploring, "Jay. . ."

He let go of her arm, but having quickly shifted to rest on his knees instead of his heels, he placed two strong hands at her waist. His hands warmed her through the cool material, and again his thumbs didn't stay still.

When she protested yet again, he implored, "Don't stop me, Robin, because this episode wins the Emmy for us! You've been brought into emergency in delirium! It's too late for me to treat you in the conventional manner. No, not this time. This time I have to use my lips. Quickly, realizing that precious seconds are slipping past, I hurry the nurses and orderlies out of the room. Then I—"

"Jeremiah Lasalle, if you show me what you would do you're going to be in worse trouble than the Kurosawa boys! Besides, the network canceled our show! You have to go back to being an engineer, and I have to . . ." She paused, only for a second, before stating the conclusion that she had to return to Caroline's house.

"You don't want to go back yet," he said, correctly interpreting that pause.

"I should."

"Because you're tired?"

"No, because . . . I should."

He had rocked back on his heels. Now he leaned forward and put his hands on her shoulders.

Robin looked up at his deeply shadowed, very beautiful and serious face. She reached a hand to his jaw, feeling another kind of nighttime shadow. The dense mat of short bristles was sensuously masculine against her palm, and now it was her thumb that grazed exploratively over firm tan skin. "Can't you be good, Jeremiah?" she asked. Immediately aware of the inconsistency between her words and action, she took her hand from his face.

"I can be very good, if I get my way," he said seductively, but in an abrupt change of mood he next suggested that they build a sand castle.

She grinned, not believing for a moment he wanted to do that. "You put up buildings during work hours; erecting a sand castle would be something of a busman's holiday, wouldn't it?"

"You won't build a castle with me?"

"Jay, you should take me back."

In seconds he was lying flat on the sand, not even protecting the back of his hair with his hands. "Robin, I don't want the night to end," he said earnestly. "You arrived on the island today, and it's like a holiday. Can't we at least stay out here and wait for the Martians to land?"

She was about to argue, but his position looked infinitely inviting. To be lying on her back on clean cool Hawaiian sand, looking up at stars, waiting for the Martians to arrive. Why not? Only because she might be tempting him to break his promise.

Again correctly interpreting her indecisive pause, he said, "What's stopping you from lying down next to me, Robin? There are no warty toads on the beach. It's safe."

"Are you sure?" She looked at him sideways.

He patted the dry sand beside him. "Use my jacket for a pillow."

"Uh-uh. If I'm going to do it, I'm going to do it right, like you are." She eased herself off the jacket and sat down next to him, then stretched her legs out and lay back.

His hand reached for hers and they entwined little fingers. That was all. No other touch. For minutes neither spoke. Then, barely above a low whisper, Jay began to sing the slow caressing words of the "Hawaiian Wedding Song."

Robin had heard this song many times, once sung by a famous pop singer at a Las Vegas show. But she had never really listened to the words. She did now, as Jay sang first in English and then Hawaiian. "*Ke Kali Nei Au.* I am waiting for thee." So beautiful, and Jay's voice, even purposely subdued, was a deep bass that added to the romance of the words.

He turned to face her when he was finished, propping himself on an elbow. "For an encore, I can do a mean rendition of the Hawaiian war chant, but not lying down."

"For an encore, would you sing the wedding song again?" Robin asked. "But wait, Jay. Before you do, I want you to promise that we'll leave afterward."

He sat up, crossing his legs Indian-fashion, and sang the song to her. She kept her eyes closed this time, not wanting to experience anything but his voice while he sang, not even the splendor of the stars. For some unknown reason, the beauty of the melody had struck a chord of melancholy in her. When the song was done, he stood up and reached a hand down to help her to her feet.

"How's your ankle?" he asked.

"Wonderful. I'd forgotten that anything had happened to it. Please don't be angry with the boys."

After brushing off the sand, he flung his jacket over his shoulder, and they walked with arms around each other's waist. When they reached the house, Robin went straight to the car and waited while he took Baxter inside. He retrieved Robin's belongings, but didn't bother to put his socks and shoes back on.

At Caroline's he walked Robin inside, kissed her chastely on the forehead and murmured good night.

She started up the stairs, then went back down and hurried after him; he was already at his car. "Jay, wait," she demanded softly. "You promised not to kiss me while we were at your house. We're not at your house anymore."

She was in his arms, and the first kiss lasted for long moments. The second did, also. "I've had such a wonderful time," she whispered when their lips parted. "I can't remember having had a lovelier evening."

"Shall we do it all again?" he returned, and when she said she'd like to, he kissed her gently. "How about right now. But we'll skip Canlis and go directly to my office."

Robin chuckled. "Good night, Jay." She let herself into the house, a smile still teasing her lips.

Just before turning off the bedside light, she looked at the Monet on the wall. She still hadn't given the painting the attention it deserved. It was wonderful, but not more wonderful than anything that had happened to her tonight. She turned the light off.

Just beginning to drift off, she heard a sound outside, as of a chair being scraped over the terrace below. She walked silently to the window, parted the draperies inches with her fingers, and looked out. Jay had meant what he'd said. He didn't want to go to sleep on this night. It was too special, too much of a holiday for sleeping. He'd moved two chairs together so he could sit on one and put his feet on the other. His hands were clasped behind his head, and he was looking seaward.

Robin touched her fingertips to her lips, then to the window glass. "Good night, Jeremiah," she whispered softly.

7

A WEEK WENT BY, during which Robin accompanied Jay to a reception given by the Philippine Consulate General and to a "topping off" party in the penthouse of a high-rise office tower, built by another structural engineering firm. On one perfect day they visited the Polynesian Cultural Center, the Bishop Museum, Chinatown and the Honolulu Zoo in Kapiolani Park.

Another day they had picnicked within sight of the fluted cliffs of Windward Oahu, relishing the enchanted island beauty and the nearness of each other. They had ridden horses into the botanic paradise of Koko Head Crater and dined that night on Caroline's chili con carne, which Jay explained had been his favorite dish since the very week she became his stepmother.

In one week, Robin had fallen in love. In another week, she was supposed to go home. Jay was urging her to extend her vacation, and she wasn't at all certain that she wouldn't give in and do it. She knew Eleanor would encourage her to stay longer, sincerely wanting her to prolong her enjoyment.

But would Eleanor really, deep down inside, fear that her place in her daughter's heart was being usurped by Caroline? That question, to which only Eleanor knew the answer, was why Robin hadn't phoned home yet. The hours speeding past were too exciting and precious to mar with worry, though.

The day before she, Jay and Caroline were to go island-hopping, Robin breakfasted with Caroline on the terrace, then swam for an hour. Afterward, she and Caroline descended on the Ala Moana Shopping Center for their first mother-daughter shopping spree. Although they were supposed to join the entire Lasalle Engineering staff for lunch, they were enjoying each other's company so much that they were reluctant to end their expedition.

Caroline insisted on buying an outfit for Robin, after which Robin insisted on doing the same for Caroline. Robin bought gifts for two friends in Las Vegas and one who lived in Boulder City, Nevada, and that moved Caroline to buy gifts for two friends who lived within five minutes of her.

"I'll get a thrill out of saying to Valerie and Nora, 'I bought this for you when I was out shopping with my daughter,'" Caroline admitted.

When they could hardly walk another yard and their arms could hold no more packages, they ceased making merchants happy and headed for the restaurant where Jay was waiting for them.

It excited Robin to know that she would be seeing him in mere minutes. As she and Caroline walked, Robin secretly relished the thought of spending an entire week with Jay. They would be on Kauai, which Jay said was his favorite island, for two days, and then they planned to go on to Maui and the big island of Hawaii.

Arriving at the restaurant, Caroline and Robin were seated and introduced to those who were already gathered. Robin was touched by the pride in Jay's tone as he briefly told her about each member of his staff. She was also moved by the purpose of the luncheon.

Hope Keating, the firm's receptionist, was returning home to Kansas after living on Oahu for only five months. Her father was critically ill and she was needed. Jay had previously explained to Robin that he wanted to give Hope a happy send-off, because she was going to have some rough times ahead of her.

Caroline had further confided that Lasalle Engineering was giving the young woman a pink-coral and gold ring, a month's pay and airfare home, as well. Among all the things Jay had done in the past week that had won Robin's admiration, not to mention her heart, this magnanimous behavior ranked foremost in her estimation.

Sitting between Jay and Dan Riley at Horatio's pewter-and-brass-filled tavern overlooking the Kewalo Boat Basin, Robin surveyed the employees of Lasalle Engineering. She was truly impressed by the camaraderie and vibrancy of the large group. Jay, it seemed, not only filled his offices with the best and the brightest people, but with the nicest.

"Little does Caroline know that you've already met the staff," Jay murmured to Robin, looking toward where Caroline sat on the other side of Dan.

"Let's keep it our secret," Robin answered, laughing, then took a bite of the freshly baked Russian rye bread that accompanied all entrées at Horatio's.

Jay leaned toward her. "This may surprise you, but I'm choosing this lunch as the best time I've had with you so far. And 'so far' covers a lot of good times."

"'So far' covers some very good times," Robin agreed, after swallowing the delicious bread. "I'm enjoying it, too, but I am surprised that it wins first place with you." She looked at him expectantly, waiting to hear his reason.

"I'm just so damned proud. Everybody's been told that you're Caroline's daughter, but everybody knows without being told that you're my sweetheart. You are, you know. Having the people I work with aware of it makes me feel like a king."

Robin's eyes became moist. She decided emphatically that she would call Eleanor that afternoon to say she was extending her trip. She had never known a man with Jay's qualities and strengths before, and she suddenly realized that the way he felt about her increased her feeling of self-worth immeasurably.

With a smile, she said, "I've thought you were a prince since a week ago when you stopped being a warty toad, but because of what you're doing for Hope I think you do deserve the status of king. I admire you, King Jeremiah Lasalle, more than you can know."

"Good. Know what I'm going to do about that?" he asked, grinning mischievously. Making her wait for the answer, he took a bite of food, chewed slowly, then dabbed at his lips with his napkin before speaking. "I'm going to cancel our dinner reservation at Champeaux's and cook for you myself tonight."

"Oh, that'll be nice. Why don't you let Caroline and me bring a tossed salad. We'll bring the wine, too."

Jay was grinning almost wickedly as he said, "I'll provide the wine. I'll make the salad. You bring a bathing suit." Then, speaking more softly, he leaned close and murmured, "I'm not inviting Caroline."

Robin took a sip of ice cold water. Putting the glass down, she looked at Jay and said, "Don't you think she'll feel left out? She was planning on having dinner with us."

"She won't feel left out. Caroline's very understanding," Jay assured her.

Robin took another bite of bread and Jay turned to speak to Hope, who was seated on his right. Dan then caught Robin's attention, telling her that he was a Don Rickles fan, and the last time he was in Las Vegas he saw the outrageously caustic comedian four times. "I also lost three hundred dollars gambling and was exhausted for a week after getting home," he grumbled.

"Next time, come and spend a little of your time and money at Eagle Garden," Robin suggested, laughing even though her mind was still on what Jay had proposed for that night.

"I hope you've been thinking about which bathing suit to wear tonight," Jay said, when Hope was engaged in conversation with someone else and Robin was through talking to Dan for the moment.

"I was thinking that Caroline should have dinner with us," Robin said firmly.

"I won't budge. You elevated me to king, and kings always get their way."

"*You* elevated yourself to king, and I . . . I just happened to have bought a bathing suit this morning," Robin informed him, chastizing herself for giving in so readily.

She envisioned herself diving into Jay's pool wearing the new bathing suit. It was not a skimpy bikini or a brazenly revealing one piece suit of the sort that makes mothers cringe and grown men blush. However, it was the most provocative bathing suit Robin had ever owned. Styled like a Grecian tunic, it was pure winter white, highlighting her satin smooth skin and revealing her womanly curves.

She imagined getting out of Jay's pool with the brief shimmery tunic clinging to her body. Jay would be holding a towel open for her, and when he wrapped her in it his arms would come around her. . . .

"Have you ever tasted *laulau*?" Jay asked.

"*Laulau?*" she asked blankly, her mind still on more erotic topics.

"It's butterfish, pork and taro leaves wrapped and steamed in fresh *ti* leaves—an island favorite. Many have said that I know my way around butterfish."

Robin refrained from laughing out loud, but she chuckled and said, "At last, I'm going to my first phony luau!"

Jay pretended to be affronted. "You're lucky I'm a king with a sense of humor. If I wasn't I'd put you in the tower for that. No, seriously, you'll love my *laulau*."

Robin thought that loving Jay's *laulau* was the least of her worries. She was excited about having dinner with him alone, without Caroline being there, also. But she was apprehensive, too.

The only thing she was sure of was that Jay made a passable *laulau*. It occurred to her that the change in this evening's plans might be meant to pave the way to lovemaking. It seemed so. They could get to bed so much more easily if they started out in Jay's dining room than if they started out at Champeaux's.

"Robin. Yoohoo, Robin," Jay said softly, and underneath the table his hand found hers on her lap.

"Yes. I'm sorry, I was dreaming." She snapped to attention, feeling very much like a servant caught daydreaming by the king. Impulsively, as if begging the king's pardon with an intimate touch, she took and held his hand tightly.

"I don't want you to worry about tonight. The same rules will apply as the last time you were in my home, if you want them to."

She let go of his hand and he discreetly withdrew it from her lap. "Well?" he asked.

"I don't know," she whispered. "I honestly don't know."

"No rush. You think about it, and let me know by word or deed. Fasten a message to Baxter's collar if you want slow dancing, or play footsies with me under the table to let me know you'd like to sit on my lap during dessert. Don't send any messages if you want it to be a hands-off experience start to finish. I'll be just as crazy about you either way. That's a promise, Robin."

He then got up and after lightly touching her shoulder began walking around the tables, stopping to talk with draftsmen, clerks, engineers, the business manager, an architect and the young errand boy.

Robin watched him move, smile, laugh, talk. With seeking fingertips she touched her shoulder to feel where his hand had last been upon her. He looked at her from across the room, standing between the chairs of huge Duke Jones and petite Myra Tsin, his golden hair appearing all the more bright for his being surrounded by black-haired people. She knew that he was as aware of her physically as she was of him. He even ran a hand over his hair now as if her concentration on him had made his very scalp tingle.

When Jay leaned down to talk to Tim Ho, whom he had described to Robin as being brilliant and shy,

Robin envisioned tracing the outline of his face with a fingertip. When he stood up, she couldn't help but think of his playful suggestion of slow dancing or having dessert while on his lap. Or both. She made a mental note to have paper and a pen in her handbag tonight so she could fasten a message to Baxter's collar. Clasping her hands together, she rested her chin on them, thinking that after dinner she and Jay would certainly become lovers.

Her joyful anticipation was marred, however, by the realization that if Jay was as much in love with her as she was with him, parting would be impossible. But equally impossible was her coming to Hawaii to live. She couldn't do that to Eleanor who needed her, Eleanor who had been her real and only mother from the day she was born. Robin could never abandon her that way—she didn't deserve to be left alone, and it would never happen. Dammit, she railed inwardly, life was too complicated. She suddenly felt like crying.

JAY STOOD by his cooking island in the gleaming white kitchen and surveyed the makings of dinner—a small but thick choice steak for grilling, greens for a salad, snow peas to be briefly steamed and potatoes. He decided to give the potatoes a head start in the microwave, then bake them for twenty minutes in the toaster oven.

He had had to call an urgent conference to re-
solve a problem concerning a project in Guam, and
because of that, preparing *laulau* was out of the
question, as was dining at a reasonable hour. But
when he'd called Robin to tell her this, apprehensive that she would suggest foregoing dinner, her
response had made him extremely happy. Not only
was she agreeable to his picking her up at eight-
thirty and their eating at nine-thirty, she informed
him that she had extended her trip by four days.

She had offered to take a cab, saying she knew
he would be beat from his long meeting, but he had
protested. He'd suggested, then, that since they
were eating so late she might prefer a walk on the
beach to a swim and said he would check the beach
out first, in case the twins had been up to their
tricks.

Robin had chuckled and said she'd be happy to
either walk or swim. She told him that Caroline
was being taken to dinner by friends, and that she
was grateful it had turned out that way because
she'd worried about Caroline feeling left out.

Feeling great relief, Jay had hung up the phone.
That Robin hadn't canceled their dinner said
something to him. She wanted to be alone with him
just as much as he wanted it.

After that night they would be in Caroline's
company for the remainder of Robin's stay. Which

was as it should be, he reminded himself. This was Caroline's big moment, her reunion with a beloved child whom she had never known. He musn't rob her of too much of Robin's time here. Already he had taken Robin away from Caroline for an entire day and half of another. But he had purposely kept away from them on two nights and three days, and it had nearly killed him to do so.

Caroline knew by now what was happening between him and Robin, of course. She'd even called him at the office to say she wouldn't mind if they went out more often without her. "I don't have to see Pearl Harbor with Robin, Jay. If you can get away for a few hours today, why don't you go instead?"

"Nonsense," he had replied. "Robin wants to be with you just as much as you want to be with her. And tonight I'm working late with Tim Ho, Dan Riley and Duke Jones. So you won't see me." Then he'd sat staring at the phone, wanting to call Caroline back and renege.

He'd had to resist canceling his appointments and dashing off in his own car to meet them at Pearl Harbor. He had worked late that night, without even interrupting the momentum of the productive hours to call Robin on the phone. He'd felt downright noble; he hadn't given Caroline so fine a gift since he'd carved a wood bowl for her at camp.

He made the salad, set the table, changed his shirt because in whisking the papaya seed salad dressing he'd flecked a drop on his sleeve, then headed for the car. Before he reached the Rolls, he did an about-face, dashing first to the garden, then back into the house to hastily put together a simple floral arrangement to adorn the table. Finally, he got into the car and set off to pick up Robin.

Robin. Robin Eagle, who made his heart soar. He'd been such a fool, having been so suspicious that he'd had her checked out by an investigator. He winced inwardly, remembering how he had interrupted Robin's reunion with her mother by harrassing her, belittling her. He'd taken her joy and turned it to anger and shame. He'd marred the beauty of Caroline's giving Robin the earrings—a gesture that he himself had instigated—by suggesting to Robin that such gifts were exactly what she had come here for.

"You toad," he muttered aloud, scowling at himself in the rearview mirror. He decided that it was only because night had fallen that he couldn't see any warts.

RAIN BEGAN TO FALL almost the moment they arrived at the house, so Jay wasn't able to use the grill.

Instead, he was pan frying the steak with a little butter, a little brandy, a generous sprinkling of coarse freshly ground pepper and a conservative pinch of dried herbs. He supposed he was creating a cross between Steak au Poivre and Steak Diane.

Actually he didn't know what he was creating, and he didn't care. With Robin in his home, the gentle patter of rain on the roof was like a drumbeat of sensuality. She'd given no clues yet as to whether tonight was hands-on or hands-off, and that created much more of a mystery than wondering how the steak would turn out.

She was in the family room, an extension of the huge kitchen, standing by the glass-topped desk framed with brushed steel. He could talk to her easily from where he was working.

"The first time I was here we only stayed outside a minute, then we went for our walk," she commented. "I really haven't had a chance to admire your home, not as much as it deserves admiring. Your glass collection is magnificent."

"Which is how I would describe you," Jay said, looking up from his cooking. She smiled and murmured thanks, but he knew that she thought he had exaggerated.

He hadn't. She was a vision, with her strawberry-blond hair falling in lush waves to her shoulders and cut in long feathery bangs that arced teasingly over her graceful brows. She was gazing at a four-sided Lalique vase that stood on the desk together with a telephone, pen holder and notepad.

Looking up at him with those wide long-lashed gray eyes that he considered to be more exquisite, more mystifying, than any art fashioned of glass or otherwise, she noted appreciatively. "Even this desk looks like art." She ran her fingers over the sculpted edge.

He refrained from answering that the true work of art in the room was her glorious self. Best to go easy on that sort of talk, he thought, giving another cautious splash of brandy to the buttery sauce simmering around the steak. What she was admiring were mere objects; Robin, on the other hand, was unique.

Wearing slacks and matching shirt of pale gray-green silk—so pale that it was like fine bone china—she was a feast for his eyes. Her skin was more suntanned than when she'd arrived on Oahu, and, as she leaned over the desk, her slacks stretched taut over her firm buttocks, he felt a sudden rush of warmth as he imagined tracing her tan line—all her tan lines—with gentle kisses. And maybe just one or two tiny love bites.

While Jay abandoned his duties as cook to get a drink of cold water, Robin came into the kitchen.

She perched on a stool at the cooking island and watched as Jay went back to moving the steak around in the pan. Baxter watched, too, with gleaming eyes, as if he suspected that these two humans had no genuine interest in food tonight and the steak was destined to end up in his bowl.

"I'd like to know two things about you, Jeremiah," Robin said.

He looked intently at her. "Are these serious questions?" he asked; he was so befuddled by her presence he really couldn't tell. When she had entered the kitchen, so many smooth textures, so much electricity, so subtle but powerful a scent had come with her that he knew only that he wanted to slip the steak into the disposal, forget the baked potatoes, let the salad wilt and take this woman to his bed. "I don't think I can handle serious questions, cooking and your presence all at one time," he said honestly.

She smiled at his admission. "They're serious, but not somber serious."

"Okay. Shoot. Question one."

"Question one," she echoed. "Why glass?"

"Haven't you ever met a man who collected glass?" he returned, giving himself time to think about the answer. He'd never been asked why he'd become a collector of glass art before, so he'd never had to express himself on the subject.

"No, or a woman, come to think of it."

"Well, we might be a rare breed, because it's an expensive and work-producing hobby. Glass needs to be cleaned, even if it's kept behind other glass. I think I collect glass because it's fragile. The better the glass, the more unpredictable its future existence. Glass can just crack for no apparent reason. It has stresses within itself."

"And you like something that can be easily broken, or that may break without provocation?" she asked, her voice becoming somewhat serious. "I don't understand, Jay, but it sounds ominous."

He put his wooden spoon down and moved to stand in front of her. Though he yearned to wind her shimmering hair round and round his hand, he didn't touch her. Until she gave him the message, he would keep his distance.

"It would be ominous if I liked people to be that way, but I don't," he said. "I like strong people, adaptors and survivors, like you."

She blushed, obviously remembering her embarrassment at having said that about herself and her mother, and he wanted to caress the glowing cheek that was half-shaded by her wealth of hair. He didn't. He wanted to say, I love you. Besides liking you, I love you, Robin.

He didn't do that, either. Instead he said, "In my work I deal with substances that are so strong you half expect them to thwart time, to be here forever. And in working with these things, to create durable structures, there's no margin for error, for vulnerability. I don't quite know how to explain this, Robin, but sometimes, after my involvement with a structure is finished, after the topping-off party and all the congratulations on a job well done, I feel deflated.

"I always like what I've built, but erecting huge buildings in a world already filled with them, buildings that take up room that might be better used for parks or just left as open space, leaves me with a bit of ambivalence. My dad felt it, too; he told me about it when I decided to follow him into structural engineering. And yes, in case you're wondering, I love being what I am. I couldn't do anything else or stop filling the world with buildings. I just have to be sure that they're beautiful and functional besides being durable, to keep the ambivalence in check. And I collect glass."

She didn't answer—not verbally. He was standing just a few inches in front of her, looking down at her upturned face. She reached forward and placed her hands on his bare forearms and trailed her fingers gently down to his wrists. They were standing very close. She rested her head on his chest and wrapped her arms around his waist.

Giving in to his desire, Jay stroked that wonderful hair, her shoulders and her back. And then he stopped, keeping his hands still against her head. He didn't know why. This was victory. She'd given her message; it was loud and clear. She was his to touch and love. And yet he hesitated. Perhaps it was because at last there was a woman in his home that he could love and be loved by for life. Or perhaps it was because he'd unburdened himself to her of a deep feeling that he'd never put into words before. Or perhaps it was the shame he felt at having wronged her, at having invaded her privacy in a most odious way and being aware of things he had no business knowing.

He couldn't rid himself of his guilty feelings, nor could he talk at this moment, either. Resting his head on hers gently, he asked her forgiveness and understanding in silence.

Robin broke the silence. "The second question," she began, gently massaging the small of his back as she spoke the few words, "is how did you get over your mistrust of me so quickly? Before we had dinner at Canlis that night, what happened to make you change your mind about me?"

Guilt, he answered to himself. *Oh, Robin, I can't forgive myself for spying on you.*

8

"WELL?" ROBIN MURMURED, turning her face to rest her cheek against Jay's chest.

He stroked her hair and replied, "Do I have to answer that one? I don't know if I can." Lifting her head so that their eyes met, Jay brushed her bangs away from her forehead and kissed her there. "Ask me why I've fallen in love with you, Robin," he continued. "I could list reasons for that all night and all day tomorrow without repeating myself once."

"Mmm, I'd cut you off, Jay, to tell you why I've fallen in love with you." Robin's tone was light, but she turned her face away from his gaze, resting against him again. The terrible reality of their situation had crept into her thoughts.

They were two people in love who had no future together. It was that simple, because Robin knew she could never share happiness with Jay if she destroyed Eleanor's sense of self-worth and purpose in the process. Should Robin abandon her mother now, Eagle Garden would ultimately fail and Eleanor would not only lose her daughter, but also the business that had been the focus of her life for nearly two decades.

No, she couldn't give her mother such pain. Robin tried to take comfort from Jay's strength and warmth, holding tightly to him for just this moment. Just for now. Pulling him closer, then closer still, she tightened her arms around his waist until their bodies were pressed against each other. Whatever the future might bring, she wanted to be his lover now. She told him so with her eyes and a whispered "I love you."

He rained kisses that were at once both tender and passionate on her head in response, before saying, "Robin . . . oh, my beautiful angel, I don't deserve you. I wish I did, but I don't."

Robin kissed his chest. By barely touching her lips to his ice blue shirt she could breathe the sweetness of him. But it wasn't enough; she needed to taste him. She turned her head and sought his strong tanned arm with her mouth, then lazily grazed the tip of her tongue along the smooth hard line of muscle.

She slowly ran her hands over his back to his waist and around so that her palms lay flat against his taut stomach. When she moved them upward over his broad chest, his breathing quickened in response. She caressed him lightly, her fingertips lingering, while her breasts swelled with desire.

"Robin . . ." He spoke in a low, husky voice; her name was almost a moan.

"I love you, Jay...I..." Her words came thickly, the sounds barely able to escape her hungry mouth.

His hands roamed her back urgently, his wide-spread fingers communicating sexual tension. Then, as though he could no longer be without her lips, he tilted her face up to kiss her.

Robin wanted him then, with all her being. Already her body was impatient for him to enter its depths. But the waiting was sweet torment.

Jay lingered at her lips, letting one kiss become the next and the next. Plunging his tongue deep, he relished how tightly she held to it. He teased at her love-swollen lips, barely parting them until she coaxed him farther.

When at last they broke apart, breathless, Robin pressed her face against his chest once again, reveling in the heady blend of his masculine scent. She felt the crispness of curls of hair beneath the cotton shirt and his small hardened nipples. Gently, very gently, she closed her teeth over one nub, and Jay moaned deep in his throat.

"Robin . . . Robin, *now*," he whispered hoarsely.

In reply she touched his chin with a fingertip, then drew the finger in an exploring line down along his throat, his chest, his stomach...until she was where she wanted to be. She stroked him softly.

Again he whispered her name, and having grasped her shoulders, he brought her to her feet, so they stood with their bodies touching in one unbroken line. "I want to look at you, Robin. I want to have all your body to feast my eyes on and then I want to taste you, be in you, be part of you . . . Robin . . . How I feel . . . I've never felt this way before. . . ."

His fingers had loosened their urgent grip as he spoke and he held her lightly, as if she were breakable, formed from delicate glass. But when his hands moved downward to cup her breasts, the chaste tenderness became hungry passion again.

Robin's eyes closed dreamily. Her lips parted in ecstasy because she knew that he would kiss one breast that ached for his lips to claim it, and then the other. And he did.

Over and over she said his name, the resonance of it filling her mind and spilling from her on short exhalations of desire. She pledged herself to him with total abandon, giving herself wholly, not questioning how much he would give or take in return.

Slipping his arms around her, he pressed his fingers into the firm curve of her buttocks, pulling her even more closely to him. He trailed soft kisses along the column of her neck, and Robin melted where she stood, thinking she would collapse with yearning.

Jay knelt to kiss her silk-sheathed thighs and then lower still. Between kisses he uttered Robin's name and stroked her now trembling legs.

She wanted no barriers between them, wanted to feel only the textures of their enflamed bodies. Looking down at Jay, kneeling before her on the hard kitchen floor, Robin could no longer hold her own weight.

She slid to the floor and entwined her arms around his throat. "I love you . . . I worship you, Jay. . . I . . . Love me . . . now." She pressed her lips to his throat, her hair falling over his shoulder. "Now."

As if in one smooth motion, Jay had one arm beneath her legs and the other around her back and was standing, holding her. She let her head fall back, her eyes closed against the brilliant kitchen light. When he dipped his head to hold one swollen nipple gentle captive, Robin grabbed his hair and cried out, her pleasure bordering on sensual pain.

Jay began to move slowly toward the bedroom. As if teasing her, he stopped now and again to tantalize her mouth or breasts. It was obvious he knew how maddeningly the flames of desire licked at

Robin's nerve endings, but he had chosen to take his time putting the fire out.

Nothing moved quickly except the rain pattering on the roof and the beating of her heart. As though mesmerized, she stood by his bed while he turned on a lamp. Nor did she move when, very slowly, deliberately, he undressed her.

When she stood naked before him, he kissed her—her mouth, her throat, her breasts—and then lifted her onto the bed. In one all-encompassing look he drank in the sight of her, his hand following the line of his gaze, coming to rest at the yearning cleft beneath the soft curling hair.

Leaving her for what seemed an eternity, he rose and undressed. When he finally eased down on the bed, straddling her, Robin reached for him, to guide him.

"No," he said softly, sensing her impatience. "There's so much of you I haven't touched, haven't kissed. I want every inch of you, Robin, inside and out."

And this, she discovered, was what she had wanted, too. Her awakening to him had only just begun, for from the very pinnacle of sensual feeling, even more desire spiraled. Desire spilled from her in abandoned utterances and cries and offerings of herself, and in return she received the exquisite sensation of feather-soft strokes of his tongue and fingers. The pulsating warmth surged through her as his own desire grew more urgent, more demanding.

Before Jay allowed his passion to explode in her, before ecstasy was abated and they rested, he had made certain that no part of her was denied. And when peace did come, he let her know with words what he'd told her with his body. "Robin, I love you. It's just the beginning. We belong to each other forever."

The rain still came down, but more gently, as if the sky's passion was spent, also. Robin listened to the gentle tattoo of water falling from the eaves and trees outside the windows, not having to answer Jay's words out loud. He already knew she felt as he did.

THEY ATE THEIR LONG-DELAYED MEAL in the cheerful breakfast nook–solarium instead of the formal dining room.

In a bowl in the center of the table were tropical flowers that even Robin didn't recognize. They drank wine and ate the salad, while in the laundry room Baxter dined on the charred steak.

Robin sat at the glass-topped table wearing one of Jay's polo shirts over her bathing suit; her silk slacks and shirt lay in a wrinkled heap in the bedroom. If the folds of the Grecian tunic caused the knit shirt to bulge unfemininely here and there, she didn't mind. She was a woman wearing her beloved's clothing for the first time, and she had discovered it to be one of the unexpected joys of love.

When Robin had confided this to Jay, he had leaped up from the table, saying, "Don't go away."

He returned with Robin's gray slacks tied shawl-fashion over his back, the legs dangling over his chest. "Feels good, and smells a little like your perfume," he said, taking a lusty deep breath.

Robin contained her laughter long enough to inform him that she never perfumed her legs. "You're just making that up," she accused him.

Watching as Jay took the pants from around his neck and draped them over the back of a chair, Robin thought fondly that she would never look at them again without remembering this night. She would keep them until the silk was aged and faded. Sometime, when she was very old, she would look at them and remember Jay. And because she was very old, and because time had healed, she would smile.

She smiled now, saying, "There are flowers everywhere in Hawaii, even on people's clothes. I'll miss the profusion of color when I'm back home."

"But you won't be away for long." His tone had suddenly become serious.

Robin didn't answer. She looked down at her plate and swallowed hard. When she did speak, she again attempted trite conversation. "Caroline tells me that the public gardens in Hilo are spectacular. I'm looking forward to seeing them, plus the black sand beaches and volcanoes. I hope we'll have enough time to see everything."

"All right, Robin. I see that you don't want to talk about where you're going to be in a month, or a year, or in ten years."

"You're right," she said softly.

"Then there's something I want to bring up about the trip to the outer islands. Will you do me one favor?"

"I'll try." Robin smiled, glad that the solemn moment was past. Sadness should not be allowed to mar this perfect night.

"Will you share a room with me instead of with Caroline?" he asked, reaching a hand out to rub his knuckles against her cheek.

She took the hand in hers and turned it so she could kiss the palm. "No," she said firmly. "And you set yourself up for that disappointment. Caroline would be horrified if I shared a hotel room with a man I'd only known a week. Can you imagine how shocked she'd be if she knew about tonight?"

"She'd be thrilled if she knew about tonight," Jay said seriously. "Do you want to know why?"

Robin didn't reply. She knew Jay was right, but she didn't want to hear why Caroline would be thrilled.

He ignored her silence and continued. "She'd think we were going to get married, which we are," he concluded.

"Jay...I...I'm going to do the dishes!" Robin stood up from the table abruptly. The chair legs rasped over the floor.

He remained seated. "No, you're not."

"Yes, I am. I insist."

"And I insist that we're going to get married. However, let's not fight over either issue. We can both get what we want. You do the dishes tonight, and we'll get married sometime in the near future."

Robin sat back down and put a hand on his arm. "Jay, your wanting to marry me is the best thing that's ever happened to me. It's also the saddest. I'm so in love with you. And there's nothing I want more than to be your wife. But I can't. I cannot leave Eleanor all alone in Las Vegas. I'm all she has. Can't you understand what that means in a life like hers?"

"Yep. I can. It's a problem, but probably not as big a problem as you think. Robin, you're creating obstacles that either don't exist or at least can be overcome. We'll find a way. You must trust our love."

Then, obviously deciding that the difficult subject had been dealt with sufficiently, he smiled a little and said, "I should take you back to Caroline's, so you can get a good night's sleep before the trip. But how are we going to justify your showing up wearing my shirt and carrying your clothes over your arm?"

"Won't Caroline be asleep?"

"She might be. Or she might be watching a late-night movie. She does that often."

"Well, do you have an iron? You can do the dishes while I try to get some of the wrinkles out."

"I've got a better idea," he ventured. "We'll leave the dishes and the ironing and go for a walk on the beach. It's been a long time since we walked by the water late at night—a whole week in fact."

Robin smiled with surprise. "That's a marvelous idea, but it's still raining."

"I know." Jay stood up first and held his hand out to her.

Standing with him, their hands joined, Robin allowed herself to think that possibly, just possibly, Eleanor might harbor a secret yen to live in paradisical Hawaii. Surely there were many Nevadans who, feeling landlocked and dust-weary, packed up and moved to the islands. Of course there were.

After poking his head out the door, Baxter refused to accompany them in the rain, so without him they walked barefoot at the edge of the sea.

The rain felt warm, but the wet sand was cool, cool enough for Jay to say, "You're going to be chilled. Let me warm you."

Held tightly in his strong, loving arms Robin listened to the mingled sounds of surf and rain. She listened to Jay's words of love and heard herself ask, "Jay, back in the house, in the kitchen, did you ask me to marry you?"

"I demanded it," he answered, hugging her fiercely.

"Well, that's what I thought. I just wanted to make sure."

"Are you saying that you will marry me?" he asked against the wet hair over her ear.

"I'm saying . . . I'm saying that I'll try to think more positively about it."

"Say yes right now and we can share a room on Kauai tomorrow night."

"No we can't. You're impossible!" She laughed, clutching his wet hair with both hands as he dipped his head down to kiss her throat.

"Well, if we can't share a room I won't be able to make love to you. I might not have a chance to make love to you even once while we're traveling with Caroline. Do you know what that means?"

"It means I'll be insane with desiring you, every hour of the trip," she replied honestly.

He didn't say a word. Letting go of her, he began to pull up the knit shirt she wore.

"Jay. . . you're not serious."

"About loving you, always!"

She stopped his hands when the bottom of her shirt was up to her breasts. "Someone will see us!" she protested.

"Not true. Even if it were a clear night, no one would be able to see us out here. And nobody will come by. Who would be foolish enough to walk on the beach in the rain, at this hour?"

She stood silently a moment, with rain falling on her, feeling warmth invade her, a fire beginning to blaze. "Nobody would be that crazy," she said softly, crossing her hands over her middle to pull the shirt over her head.

Jay made a blanket of their clothes on the sand and lay down on his back. "I've never been rained on while in this position," he said. "It's lovely. Be my umbrella, Robin."

Without question, she knelt astride him and eased herself down gently. Despite the rain the fire was still there in her. They quenched the flames quickly, Robin sitting erect, her head tilted back, the warm Pacific rain gently sluicing down her throat and breasts.

ROBIN'S HAIR WAS STILL DAMP when she slid into the passenger seat of the Rolls. At least she was no longer wearing Jay's shirt over her bathing suit, she thought gratefully. While she had basked in a steamy shower, Jay had pressed her slacks and shirt.

Feeling reasonably presentable, she smiled to herself. Here she was going home to Caroline after being out much too late on a date, and like any daughter she was feeling a little guilty, a little naughty.

"I hope you won't be exhausted in the morning," Jay said. "I wish I could change our flight to a later hour, but there isn't anything available."

"Don't worry about me. I'll be fine," Robin said. Then she sneezed.

"Bless you. If you get a cold I'll hate myself for taking you out in the rain."

Robin laughed. "You don't get colds from being out in the rain. You get colds from cold germs." But she sneezed again.

"Bless you again. Do you need a Kleenex? There's a pack in the glove compartment."

"Thanks, I do." Robin opened the glove compartment and a small light went on.

"Wait, I'll get it for you!" The insistence in Jay's tone surprised her. He quickly reached a hand to the glove compartment, apparently trying to cover the opening.

"That's okay. I'll find it," Robin said, perplexed at this behavior.

"Robin, I'll—"

"Jay, watch the road!" He'd been so intent on getting the pack of tissues for her that his gaze had strayed a moment too long. He'd gone over the double yellow line on the curving road. As he maneuvered back into his lane, with both hands now on the wheel, Robin peered into the glove compartment and reached for the Kleenex. She could see the small unopened package of tissues, but it was underneath an envelope from which a photograph protruded.

She could just see the top of the picture, but it was enough for her to recognize the subject. Keith's hair was reddish, worn in a way she was very familiar with, and even before the words *That's Keith* formed in her uncomprehending mind something lurched painfully inside her. Some quick chilling fear stunned her. She wanted desperately to close the glove compartment and pretend she'd never opened it.

"Here, I'll get that for you," Jay said quickly, bringing his hand to the open door of the small but lit compartment.

Robin moved her hand around his and withdrew the envelope. Before he could say a word she was holding the picture of herself and Keith. There was a letter in the long envelope but she didn't bother to extract that.

She was numb, but in a voice as even as the hum of the Rolls's motor she said, "Stop the car."

"No."

"I want to get out."

"Don't be silly, Robin. I can't let you out here. I'm sorry that you saw that. I . . ."

She turned and stared at him, asking, "You what? Do you want to offer some explanation? Do you think there's anything you can say that will make it be all right? Can you say something that will make me not care that you hired an investigator, that you had me . . . spied upon?"

"No, of course not," he said softly.

"No, of course not," she echoed scornfully. "You're right, though, I can't get out of the car here. I have to let you take me home. But please have the decency not to talk to me about anything!"

"If we talk, you might understand."

"No! Leave me in peace!"

He complied. They drove in silence. Robin stared out her window, one fist on her lap and the other at her mouth.

Jay stopped the car in Caroline's driveway and turned to face Robin. "I did what I felt I had to do at the time," he said. "It was a mistake. I've been sorry about it almost from the moment I met you. I even thought of telling you about it, to get it off my chest."

"I'll bet you did!" She hurled the words at him, her nostrils flaring in renewed rage at his words. "The first afternoon, in the swimming pool, you must have felt like letting me know that you were on to me, that you knew I'd been involved with someone who was deeply in debt! Why didn't you bring it out in the open when Caroline was with us? If you'd shown her that . . . that damned letter, and whatever others you have, you could have prevented my getting the jewelry, don't you think?"

He shook his head and compressed his lips fiercely, looking away from her. Then, facing her and fixing an intent gaze on her condemning eyes, he said, "Oh, Robin, honey, don't do this. It's senseless. Believe that I'm sorry, and forgive me. I am. I'm so sorry, but what I did before I met you is history. It doesn't change how we feel about each other now."

"Like hell." She said the two words in a monotone, but with cold precision.

Jay bowed his head as if defeated, and for a second she felt a tug of sympathy for him. She banished the feeling, keeping her emotions bound so tightly by outraged dignity that she couldn't be touched by any other feeling. He'd spied on her. Some stranger had watched her for pay, reporting the intimate details of her life to Jay. He probably even knew what she ate for breakfast.

It was too much—too much to take in and forgive all in one night. It was too much to forgive ever.

"I want to ask a favor of you," she said, her hand already on the door handle.

"Don't ask me to stop loving you, to give up on us, because I can't," he said quietly.

She ignored that. He could give up on them whenever he liked; she had already done it. "I don't want you to come with us tomorrow. If I could, I'd go back to Nevada immediately. Obviously I can't. Caroline wouldn't understand. I don't want to hurt her, ever, in any way. But you can call first thing in the morning and say there's some work that you have to attend to. She'll believe you."

He reached his hand toward her and she flinched. Gazing at her for a long moment, he nodded. "Yes, I'll do that."

"Thank you." She reached for her door handle, but then turned back to face him. "That's how you knew that my mother was in a wheelchair, isn't it?"

"I guess. I don't . . . I don't remember, really," he replied.

Robin felt that he was being honest, that he was tugging at his memory for the exact moment when he found out. He looked devastated. Sympathy for him welled up in her again, and again she quelled it. "Is there anything else you need to know about me?" she demanded. "What I wear to bed, for instance?"

"No, don't be ridiculous," he answered in a low tone.

"Pardon me for being ridiculous! It's not every day I find out that I've been investigated! I'm a little flustered!"

She was about to get out of the car, but Jay's hand suddenly gripped her arm. Shocked that he dared to touch her, she gritted her teeth and whipped her head around to glare at him.

Jay steeled himself in the face of her fury and did what he knew must be done. "Robin, your birth father is dead. He died a long time ago. I wanted to tell you, I was waiting for the right time to do it."

This said, he let go of her arm though his hand lingered for one moment in a caress. A sob broke from Robin's throat as she clutched the door handle with a shaking hand. She didn't know if she was grieving for the father who had died before she could know him, for herself, or for Jay. Jay's voice had carried his agony right to her heart. Still, she couldn't respond to him. There would be no solace for either of them.

"Robin, I love you."

She got out of the car, and without looking back went inside the house. Ten minutes passed before she heard the car drive off.

9

SOMETIMES ROBIN THOUGHT she would scream if Caroline didn't stop talking about Jay. She had mentioned him at least twenty times on the flight to Kauai. But at last they landed on the Garden Island and set off for the magnificent Princeville, where they had reserved a cottage with an ocean view.

Before going in for dinner, they relaxed on the terrace, drinking pineapple daquiris and eating spicy teriyaki *puupuus*. A Hawaiian entertainer played the ukulele and sang for them.

"Jay has a marvelous singing voice, you know," Caroline remarked.

"I suppose he would," Robin answered, not wanting to lie, but unwilling to admit that Jay had sung to her.

"He can act, too. In high school plays he always had a lead role. As hard as his college studies were, he still took the time to be in a few student productions. But singing is his real love. People hear Jay and they invariably say he could have been a successful entertainer."

"Did George sing?" Robin asked, hoping Caroline would switch from talking about her stepson to her husband.

"Couldn't carry a tune. But Jay! With his looks and that talent he couldn't have missed. It's amazing to me that he didn't decide to give show business a whirl," Caroline mused.

"Amazing," Robin agreed dryly. At least she was no longer on Oahu, she thought thankfully. Now that she and Caroline were on their outer island trip, there was at least some distance between herself and Jay. A few miles of ocean could create an aura of vast space. Not that that helped get him out of her mind, especially with Caroline going on and on about him.

Kauai was possibly more beautiful than any other place on Earth. Robin tried to appreciate it, but it wasn't easy when her spirit was heavy as lead. She tried to keep up a cheerful front for Caroline's sake, but one incident in particular nearly gave away the deception.

They were walking on the beach at Hanalei early their first morning on Kauai, when Robin was startled to see an elderly man in a loud Hawaiian shirt apparently filming them. She shuddered inwardly and looked away. A moment later, the man lowered the camera, and Caroline smiled at him, saying, "You should have warned us! I would have held my stomach in."

"I hoped you don't mind," he responded. "I like to get people in my scenic shots. And don't worry, I didn't get your stomach. The folks back in Omaha will just see the profiles of two beautiful sisters."

"Thank you, and we don't mind at all. Enjoy your stay," Caroline said graciously.

They strolled on. "Imagine!" Caroline exclaimed with a chuckle. "He knew that we were mother and daughter. We look enough alike that he could tell. That makes me feel so good. It's funny, though, to think that strangers—the folks back in Omaha—will get to witness this part of our reunion."

"Yes, it is," Robin murmured, her stomach still churning from her initial reaction to the stranger. She didn't think she'd ever see another camera and not remember that someone had once stalked her, photographed her, jotted down the places she went and the names of the people she saw. In her mind's eye she pictured a private detective, tough looking and hard as nails.

"You're quiet," Caroline commented. "Any particular reason?"

"Mmm. It's probably the peacefulness of Kauai that's making me thoughtful."

"You aren't missing Jay, are you?"

"Heavens, no. What makes you ask?"

"Shameless maternal nosiness. It's no secret from anybody that you two have fallen in love, Robin, unless you haven't admitted it to yourself yet."

Robin gave no answer.

"I may have realized it before you did," Caroline mused. "I woke up just after dawn last Saturday, the morning after you'd arrived. I was so excited about your finally being here that I hadn't slept very well. I looked outside and saw Jay asleep on the terrace. He looked like something the cat had dragged in, wearing pretty much what he'd had on at Canlis except he didn't have any socks on. I wondered why on earth he would have been sleeping out there, but then it hit me. He wanted to be near you.

"When I went outside and tried to wake him, he opened one eye, which has always been Jay's way of greeting the world, and said 'Caroline, I'm . . .' That was all, and then he was staring up at your window, grinning like a lovesick fool. I could have sworn his shoes weren't touching anything but air when he finally got up and left.

"What he'd meant to say, of course, was, 'Caroline, I'm in love.' It was written all over him. I've never seen Jay like that before, as if he'd just come to life for the first time. I stood there watching him go, and thinking about you two, then I went inside to make the coffee. Robin, *my* feet didn't quite touch the ground, either."

By the time Caroline finished speaking, Robin's face was flushed. She was flustered. Now, on top of everything else that was making her miserable, she would feel guilty for dashing Caroline's hopes. She had to confess that the romance was over, that everyone involved could go back to walking with his or her feet on the ground. And Caroline would be terribly disappointed.

But before Robin could formulate the best way to break the bad news to Caroline, the older woman began to talk again. "Eleanor will be the real mother of the bride, of course. But when the big day comes, it's going to be the highlight of my life, I can tell you."

Shocked, Robin stood rigidly still and blurted out a passionate denial. "Caroline, I'm *not* going to marry Jay. It...it never even came up. We're *not* in love. I'll admit that we thought we were, but it's over...completely over! Jay didn't stay on Oahu because he had work to do, he stayed because I asked him not to come with us. If he were here, I wouldn't be! And now, please...*please*, Caroline, let's stop talking about him all the time!"

Caroline looked stunned. "Oh, I'm sorry.

I'm...I'm so obtuse! Robin, forgive me for not seeing the signs. But you seemed to be having such a good time. Oh, darling, what happened? Tell me. I'm sure it's nothing that can't be ironed out."

Robin shook her head, her eyes shut and her teeth clenched together. When she opened her eyes, she saw Caroline looking sympathetic, but obviously not believing that the romance was really over. "It's not something that can be ironed out or dealt with in any way except to have it be over!" she cried, angered by Caroline's refusal to accept the truth. "I can't tell you what happened, so please don't ask me to. I wouldn't do anything to damage the relationship that you two have, but don't pretend to yourself that we'll get back together. We won't. Not ever," she finished more softly.

Caroline smiled a little, although she looked very sad and spoke compassionately. "You're still too young to predict what will happen in 'ever,' Robin. If Jay said or did something thoughtless, you must understand he's moody at times. It comes from working too hard and having too many people waiting for him to make major decisions. He's always under stress. You may not realize it, but Lasalle Engineering is one of the largest structural engineering firms in the entire Pacific. And since Jay took over, the company's contracts have practically doubled. He—"

"*Mother*, he—" Robin stopped herself, swallowing hard. "I'm sorry I shouted," she said. "And I'm sorry that I . . . that . . . well, I'm just sorry."

"No, say it. You're sorry that in the heat of the moment you called me Mother. But don't be. Robin, if the word slips out once in a while I'll enjoy it without expecting it to become a habit, and neither of us need be embarrassed by it. And it doesn't diminish your loyalty to Eleanor, my darling. Nothing will do that, ever. That part of 'ever' I can and will predict with great faith."

Robin reached a hand out to touch Caroline's arm. "I know," she said. "I am sorry for shouting, though. I guess we just had our first mother-daughter traumatic scene."

Caroline beamed. "We did, and we survived it admirably. Now let me tell you something, Robin. I love Jay as much as I love you. I raised him, and I know him as well as I know any human being. He's good through and through. So whatever happened that caused you to put him out of your life, or to think that you have, you don't have to protect me from knowing about it. Confide in me or not as you wish, but you won't jeopardize Jay's place in my heart. Nothing can do that. He is my child, just as you are Eleanor's, and I'm always immensely proud of him. He couldn't do anything that he would have to be ashamed of—not very much ashamed, anyway."

"He had me investigated," Robin said calmly. "He hired a detective who followed me and took photographs and did whatever else detectives do. The findings were reported to Jay."

Caroline's mouth was open, but she wasn't saying anything.

"It was to protect you from me. He thought I was coming here to meet you because you were rich," Robin concluded.

"I have to sit down," Caroline said weakly.

They sat facing the untroubled bay. With their arms encircling their knees, they mirrored each other's pose. To their left were the lush cliffs of the Na Pali Coast. Caroline looked in that direction, musing, "A hermit lived over there for many, many years. He'd been a doctor before he walked away from society. Right now I feel like running away, too, and hiding from what I've done."

"What you've done? This has nothing to do with you," Robin protested.

"Oh, yes it does. I'm not saying that Jay didn't exercise poor judgment, but I was the cause of it. Robin, you know how dependent I was on my husband, don't you?"

"You were a product of your generation," Robin said, defending Caroline.

"Thanks, but that's no excuse. And not all women of my generation fit into that particular mold. When George died, Jay appointed himself my guardian of sorts. What I'm really guilty of is having liked being watched over. Let's face it—it's easier that way. Once you're used to being taken care of, taking care of yourself seems like hard work. Just the thought of it is scary."

"I understand everything you're saying, but it doesn't change anything," Robin said. "I feel . . . I feel that he's done something underhanded and ugly to me."

"He has, but can't you forgive? Has he asked you to?"

"Yes, but I can't."

Caroline sighed. "Well, I do sympathize. Discovering that your privacy has been so thoroughly invaded must have been devastating. I'm glad Jay had the courage to tell you, though."

It was Robin's turn to sigh before speaking. "He didn't," she said. "I found out on my own. If he'd told me at the outset I might have been able to accept it, or at least forgive him. But, Caroline, I can't love a man who would let a lack of trust be at the core of our relationship. Jay didn't even tell me about the investigation when . . . when human decency demanded that he really should have."

She'd almost mentioned her birth father, but then realized that was a topic for another time. She wouldn't burden Caroline with that sadness now.

"I'm not going to ask you any more questions or give any advice," Caroline vowed, her tone revealing just how hard keeping that promise would be. "I'm staying completely out of it. Not another word to you—or to Jay—on the subject. Just know that I love you both."

"I do," Robin said softly. Then she said, "Caroline, let's not let what happened between Jay and me spoil this trip, not even slightly. Let's have a wonderful time. I've been feeling awful, but I'm not going to anymore. And don't you feel bad, either. We're so lucky to have this time to spend together—let's not waste it on regrets about anything. Okay?"

Caroline put a hand on Robin's knee. "I always thought to myself that Eleanor would do an award-winning job of parenting," she said. "All your attitudes prove me right."

Robin smiled. "Take a little credit yourself," she suggested. "I have your good genes."

"Not just mine," Caroline said. "Honestly, if you weren't as courageous as you are, you might be leery of meeting your birth father after all this misery."

Robin turned away momentarily, then looked at Caroline. The time was now. She couldn't be evasive or secretive, as Jay had been with her.

"He's dead, Caroline. Jay found that out in his investigation," she said gently.

Caroline buried her face in the circle of her arms and began to sob. Robin simply held her.

THE LAST DAYS of her trip were spent back on Oahu, at Caroline's. Jay's absence was painfully obvious during every hour of every day. When Caroline got a long-distance call from him the first evening and reported that he'd gone to New Zealand on business, Robin thought she might be able to relax. But she couldn't. She was constantly aware that he might come back at any moment, and she wasn't sure how she'd respond if he did.

Jay didn't come back, however. Robin made a herculean effort to have a good time for four days, then she left.

Caroline cried a little at the airport, laughing at the same time and saying that she'd promised herself she wouldn't cry. "I hope that what happened between you and Jay won't keep you from coming back to see me," she said.

"Of course it won't. And you'll come to see me, too. Caroline, even if I could have known what would happen here, I would have come to meet you. Not for the world would I have missed this reunion. We won't leave each other's lives again."

Caroline gave up all attempt to be stoic then, and cried openly.

While the pilot gave a folksy report on Las Vegas's weather, Robin wondered if she would tell Eleanor about Jay. Most likely not. There was no reason to upset her, too.

It was midday when the plane descended in a path that gave Robin a full view of Las Vegas's famed strip. Glitzy signs emblazoned the sky. Tubes of neon screamed the names of entertainers who would be onstage come night, while on the ground taxis made relentless journeys from the strip to the airport and back again.

As Robin prepared to deplane she noticed that many of her fellow passengers fairly radiated anticipation. Even though they had to know the odds were stacked against them, they were convinced they were going to make a killing in the casinos. She reflected that in three or four days these people would go back home feeling a little dejected and a little foolish for having gambled away their hard-earned money.

Robin wondered if Jay was right about Las Vegas. Maybe it was a depressing place. And because she came from a city that capitalized on greed, maybe he had been somewhat justified in mistrusting her. He had only been trying to protect Caroline in any way he could.

No! She frowned in disdain at herself, at her weakness. She was rationalizing. Out of a desire to be able to regain what she'd lost, she was searching for reasons to forgive the unforgivable.

What Jay had done to her could never be made right. It still made her cringe to think of a stranger watching her move through the hours of an ordinary day. She didn't know the extent of the investigation and had chilling moments of wondering about it. Perhaps she'd been watched while she shopped for groceries or made a deposit at the bank. In some office here in Las Vegas there must still be a file on her, perhaps with pictures in it. The thought made her flesh crawl.

"Well, hello! Welcome back! Aren't you nice and suntanned!"

Leaning down to hug and kiss Eleanor, Robin returned her mother's cheery greeting with, "Hi! Mom, you look wonderful! Let me see you! Is this the same Eleanor Eagle I waved goodbye to just eighteen days ago?"

Robin was truly surprised. Eleanor was not only wearing an entirely new and very feminine outfit, she had a new hairdo and lip color, too, and she smelled of a subtle, sweet-scented cologne. Looking more closely, Robin saw that her mother was even wearing a bit of eye shadow and mascara. Eleanor looked five years younger and mysteriously happy.

"I'll bet you're going to tell me that business has been wonderful and that you got along just fine without me," Robin ventured.

"It has been, and I did. I almost called to tell you to stay another week."

Robin thought that another week would have been more than she could bear. She summoned enthusiasm. "Great! I'm glad things went so well. But business being good doesn't account for the changes I see in you. What's up?"

"Oh, nothing you have to know about this very minute."

That was an evasive answer, if Robin had ever heard one. She gave her mother a scrutinizing look, but Eleanor's features remained unrevealing as she and Robin waited for the suitcases.

At first, all Robin had observed about her mother was that she looked lovely. Now that she'd been on the ground a few minutes, she realized that Eleanor was here alone. Pat, an Eagle Garden employee who acted as Eleanor's driver when necessary, wasn't at the airport. Eleanor wasn't able to drive, so the question remained as to how she'd gotten here. "Where's Pat?" Robin asked.

"She didn't bring me here . . . someone else did. And then left."

"Left you here alone? Why?" Robin couldn't comprehend this.

Eleanor was staring toward the baggage carousel. She looked to Robin like a woman intent on keeping her secrets until they were dragged out of her.

"You're full of mystery today," Robin chided, smiling affectionately. She bent down and kissed her mother again. "You also look beautiful."

The suitcases arrived, and Robin lifted them off the carousel. She had packed sparingly for the trip and was returning home with little more than what she'd taken with her. There were a few additions: some presents, a few new items of clothing, several pieces of jewelry and a lot of emotional pain.

She'd given the plant in the clay dove to Mailia, Caroline's housekeeper.

"Is Pat at the nursery?" Robin asked. Although she was perplexed about Eleanor's being left here alone, she was glad to be the one asking questions. It was only a matter of time, though, before Eleanor would ask for details about the trip.

"Pat's at home," Eleanor said. "She had an emergency appendectomy the day after you left. She was very sick."

"Oh, no! Oh, poor Pat! And you were without both of us! Mom, I would have come right home if I'd known Pat was in the hospital!"

Robin felt sick herself, thinking of how hard the past days must have been on Eleanor. If she was her mother's first support, soft-spoken and efficient Pat was the second.

"Don't worry—she's recovering very nicely. I talked to her this morning and she said to give you her love," Eleanor assured her as they turned to leave the airport.

"I just don't know how you managed," Robin said ruefully. Eagle Garden had good employees, but no one else with Pat's capabilities.

"Well, we have someone new. He came just at the right time—the day after Pat got sick—as if it were fated. And he works harder than any two men ever could. It all worked out. Now then, tell me, how did it go? What did you do besides get to know Caroline?"

"I had a good time. We did a lot of sight-seeing and shopping. I bought you some things, but nothing as nice as the new dress you're wearing. Caroline sent you a gift, too, and there's a letter with it that I didn't read. But, Mom, tell me what's been going on while I was away. I'm dying of curiosity. Who drove you here, and why did he or she leave you?"

"I'm not saying a word about myself until you really tell me about Hawaii," Eleanor insisted.

"You're being awfully difficult and it's not fair, especially when I'm worn out from flying. But you win—I'll talk first," Robin capitulated. She rattled off the obvious things: Hawaii is paradise, the greens are greener there and the mountains look like painted illustrations of fairy-tale countries.

"There are flowers everywhere," she said. "Kauai is called the Garden Island, and to me it was the most beautiful. The sunsets and rainbows take your breath away. Waikiki has wall-to-wall hotels, of course. And, let's see, oh ... Caroline's house is exquisite. She has a wonderful collection of original Impressionist art. There was a Monet in my bedroom, if you can believe it."

They were outside now, and Robin said she would get the van while Eleanor waited with the suitcases.

"When I get back, you'd better be prepared to talk. Otherwise I'm going to zoom off and leave you here," Robin threatened jokingly.

Eleanor probably saw right through her, thought Robin as she put the van in reverse. She couldn't figure out what was going on with her mother, though. It was all very strange—the new clothes, makeup, cologne and hairdo. Robin reflected that Eleanor *never* changed her hairstyle, and she took the time and effort to shop for new clothes only when she was tired of Robin's nagging at her to do so.

When they were in the van together, Eleanor said, "What's his name? How'd you meet him? What went wrong?"

Robin sighed and slumped in her seat. "And I thought I was being such a good actress."

"You were, darling. For two whole minutes I didn't know that anything had happened."

"Jay. His name is Jay. He's Caroline's stepson, and . . . and I can't tell you any more. I'm not ready to talk about it yet."

Eleanor put her hand on Robin's arm, saying, "You don't ever have to talk about it, if you don't want to. If you do, I'll listen. You know where to reach me, and my listening hours are flexible."

"Thanks. Hey, have I told you lately that I love you?" Robin asked softly. She did love her mother, and despite the assurance about a new employee who was worth two men, it still upset her to think that Eleanor had been without her and Pat simultaneously. "What's our new man's name? Where did you find him?" she asked.

"Curly. Curly Gibbs. He walked in off the street. Robin, we're in love."

Robin had to concentrate very hard on driving sanely for a few moments. Her mother's succinct statement had hit her like a truck. She didn't know if she could trust herself to respond—she would probably babble—so she didn't say a word.

"Are you all right?" Eleanor asked, looking at her intently.

Robin nodded.

"You don't look all right. Do you think you should pull over?"

Robin shook her head.

"Do you want me to tell you all about it, or should I keep quiet and give you time to recover?"

"Mother...speak! Stop torturing me and tell me everything that's happened."

Eleanor did. Robin learned that Curly Gibbs was single, and that he was once an Army sergeant. He'd retired twelve years ago, at the age of thirty-eight. He'd had several jobs since leaving the Army, but hadn't worked recently. He'd traveled all over the world, both in and out of the service. He had a nice face, a good build, was going gray but was physically fit, and he didn't even need glasses yet. He also sported three patriotic tattoos on his arms.

"I always thought tattoos were silly at best, but I must say that I've grown to like the bald eagle on his left biceps," Eleanor said fondly.

Robin felt faint. She drove extremely carefully and thus a little too slowly. Someone honked twice, and she moved into the slow lane. Her mother didn't say anything more for a while. Robin didn't say anything, either. She wondered silently, instead, why Curly Gibbs had never married. Hadn't she read once that bachelors over the age of thirty-five were definitely not husband material? Yes. She had. But Eleanor hadn't said anything about marrying this particular old bachelor. Thank heavens.

Finally, Eleanor broke the silence. "You don't have to look like you've seen a ghost, Robin. I know it's shocking that I have a boyfriend, but it's not the end of the world. And Curly's a fine man. I consider myself blessed, because the man I love loves me. I have to pinch myself sometimes to make sure I'm not dreaming up all this excitement and happiness. It was preceded by a long dry spell, Robin."

Robin swallowed and found her voice. There were tears in her eyes, because Eleanor had sounded so hurt when she said that her having a boyfriend wasn't the end of the world. "Mom, I'm sorry. Please don't misinterpret. It's just so sudden. This isn't something that happened gradually. I've only been gone a short while, and it doesn't seem long enough for you to have fallen in love."

"It was long enough for you to fall in love," Eleanor reminded her, but in a sympathetic tone.

Robin nodded, swallowed hard again and dabbed at her eyes with the heel of her palm. "Yes, but . . . but you've never . . . I mean, you don't fall in love as often as I do, and I almost never do!"

"And when you do, you get hurt," Eleanor said. "So you're worried that I'll be hurt. I won't be, Robin. I've complete confidence in Curly's love and integrity."

Integrity. Robin said the last word over in her mind. If ever a word could sting . . .

"Of course you do," Robin said, vividly recalling a magical night, a night when she held a panda plant on her lap while telling Jay that she had complete faith in his integrity. She forced herself to get past this cruel memory and concentrate on what she saw as potential pain in Eleanor's life. How could Curly, who lusted for travel and adorned his body with patriotic tattoos, make a commitment to this dear, intelligent, good woman? Eleanor was nearly ten years older than he was and confined to a wheelchair.

Rapidly occurring questions toppled over each other in Robin's mind. She imagined a dozen different scenarios, all of which ended with Eleanor's being hurt.

"I might as well tell you that he's going to move in with me at the end of the month," Eleanor said. "He's renting a place now, and it seems a waste of money to go on doing that because he's at my house so much of the time. He's been driving me to work and then back home and staying for dinner in the evening, so he's hardly ever at the apartment. He's paid up for three more weeks, so we'll wait until then. I've ordered some new furniture—a dinette set, a man-sized armchair and ottoman and a bed. Robin, I'm sure you're mortified by my acting this way at my age, but try to be understanding. Love is making me do it."

Again there was silence. Robin was digesting it all and trying desperately to think positively. Eleanor looked at her and smiled. "Now you tell me something about Hawaii," she said firmly. "I know what you don't want to talk about, but there are a lot of other things you can talk about."

Robin wanted to comply, but instead of launching into praise of Hawaii she stifled a sniffle and a shiver and in silence kept her eyes on the road.

"Oh, Robin, come on. Honey, talk," Eleanor pleaded.

"You're a tough act to follow," Robin murmured. Then she looked at Eleanor, really looked at her.

Eleanor was a vision of contentment; she looked truly like a woman in love. And if she was in love and happy today, wasn't that worth any hurt that would come tomorrow? Robin asked herself this, fervently hoping that she could come to believe the answer was yes.

All love affairs were not the same. All endings to love affairs did not bring the same amount of pain. Eleanor might be philosophical enough to easily weather whatever storm she had to face. There might not even be a storm. It was possible that Curly would make Eleanor happy for the rest of her life, or he might walk out of her life with amicable goodbyes all round and no hard feelings.

Robin was trying to think positively and be as supportive as possible, but the questions that had flooded her mind a few minutes earlier had not disappeared. They'd taken root and would stay until they were satisfactorily answered. She even thought she might be able to find out more about Curly on her own, if she watched for clues carefully enough and did a little investigating.

Some things she could find out just by asking questions. She began with, "What's his real name? He can't have Curly written on his birth certificate." If it did become necessary to look into his past, knowing his real name would be helpful.

"Curtis. Curtis Paul Gibbs."

Robin mumbled that name to herself. Curtis Paul Gibbs. It sounded reassuring.

"What's Jay's real name?" Eleanor asked softly.

Robin took her right hand off the steering wheel and placed it on the seat between them. Eleanor took her hand. Robin held on to her mother for dear life, because hearing Eleanor say Jay's name had made her heart crumble a little bit more. It hurt so much, so unbearably much. Just his name being said could make her feel as if she couldn't go on. Just the image of his face, flashing across her tormented mind . . .

After a long moment of silence, Robin said, "Jeremiah. I'll tell you about him and about what happened . . . someday."

"Someday," Eleanor echoed softly.

"How do you know that he only has three tattoos?" Robin asked abruptly. "Have you . . . umm . . . ."

"I sure have. Only three."

"Well, that's a relief!" Robin burst out laughing, and Eleanor joined in. They were still chuckling when Robin pulled the van into the lot behind Eagle Garden.

"You'll be okay," Eleanor said firmly. "You'll get over your heartbreak, and you'll be just fine."

"I hope so, Mom," Robin said. "Anyhow, I'm trying." She wiped her eyes, looking out the van's window. Curtis "Curly" Gibbs was coming out through the nursery's back door to greet them.

10

SEVERAL WEEKS PASSED, and Curly did not go away. Eleanor hadn't exaggerated his usefulness at Eagle Garden. He had a quick grasp of things and a natural bent toward growing plants, though he'd never been in this line of work before. And he was worth two ordinary employees when it came to hard labor.

Robin supposed she should be grateful to him, for many reasons. He had made Eleanor blossom, and Robin delighted in the transformation. Ironically, he even took her mind off what had happened in her own life. She had not done anything to find out answers to her questions, but she wasn't ready to give Curly her trust and her blessing.

Work was demanding. There were moments of respite when Robin didn't think about Jeremiah Lasalle or Curtis Gibbs. But at night, when she was home alone, she thought about Jay and she hurt. Finally she decided that she needed an afterwork activity. As she didn't feel like being sociable yet, it would have to be a solitary pursuit.

She decided to paint the interior of her house. Starting with the kitchen and breakfast nook, she'd progress until the cream-colored walls were all brighter... or more somber; she couldn't decide which. She went to a shopping mall still unsure of a color but determined not to leave without paint.

"Black," she muttered to herself. Inside the store, she smiled brightly and said she'd like to see a color wheel.

HER SMALL HOME was rapidly becoming a feast of blues—a careful blending of larkspur, delft and Cote d'Azur. The Cote d'Azur was darker than the delft and lent drama to the living room and dining area.

"You're mad to do all this yourself!" Eleanor exclaimed, wheeling herself carefully around the painting paraphernalia in the middle of Robin's living room.

"It's therapy," Robin said.

"But you're working too hard. Decorating your home is therapy, all right, but you could have hired someone to do the actual labor for you. You haven't relaxed for one day since your trip."

"There's no such thing as working too hard. Ask Curly," Robin countered. Whatever flaws he might have—and Robin had to admit that she hadn't detected any—Curly was the soul of industry. For that trait alone she admired him, and he treated Eleanor like a queen.

"We're going on a trip," Eleanor said. "Curly loves Dixieland jazz, so we're going to New Orleans. If you want, we'll wait until you get the house done. But we'd like to go next week."

Robin put her brush down. On her knees in front of her mother, she rested her arms in Eleanor's lap. She always did that when there was something very important to be discussed. "Mom, are you eloping?" she asked.

"Of course not. I'm going on a short vacation. I wouldn't get married without you being there, just as I hope you won't get married without having me in attendance, genteely weeping into my hanky."

I won't get married, period, Robin thought. She put her head on her folded arms. Eleanor stroked her hair, just as she had when Robin had been a child.

"I worry about you," Robin admitted.

"I know, and I worry about you. It comes from loving each other."

"You've never gone away, not since the accident. In your own home and at the nursery, things are organized for your comfort. I'm worried that there will be stresses you're not used to, maybe more stresses than the trip is worth. And you're going away with someone you didn't even know two months ago."

"I'm going away with someone who loves me, and what's this nonsense about stress? Since when couldn't I, or you for that matter, square off with stress and leave it lying flat on its worthless back?"

Robin had to laugh. She sat back on her heels and said, "You're right! Oh, are you ever right! And you're going to have a marvelous time! I— Wait here!" She interrupted herself and then got up to dash off to her bedroom.

"Slow down! You almost tripped over the paint can!" Eleanor complained, although Robin, in her rush to get to her room, hadn't come within two feet of the open can.

She came back with a jade necklace that had a large flawless diamond at its apex. "This will look stunning with your bronze silk dress," she said.

"It will," Eleanor agreed. "And when I'm wearing it I can swing the diamond back and forth in front of Curly and say, 'You're getting sleepy. Your eyelids are heavy. Close your eyes. Go deeper into the trance. Deeper, Curly, deeper. Now ask me to marry you.'"

"Hasn't he asked you yet?" Robin was surprised that he hadn't; he obviously adored Eleanor. "Here, let's try this on you now," she said, moving behind the wheelchair.

As she fastened the clasp of her birth mother's chain around Eleanor's neck, Robin felt both joy and pain. The joy she felt was twofold. She remembered Caroline doing this for her on the first night of their reunion, and she felt a rush of happiness at having found her. She also rejoiced with Eleanor in her reawakened womanliness. Eleanor had found happiness, and Robin was beginning to suspect it would last. "He'll pop the question on the trip," she said. "You'll see." She hoped she was right.

Then, still standing behind the chair, she reached her arms around Eleanor and rested her head on her mother's. She needed physical closeness with someone to lessen the pain welling up in her heart. She was trying so hard to put Jay out of her life, but she couldn't even secure the clasp of this necklace without remembering vividly the one night she had worn it. It was the night of magic, when Jay had made her fall in love with him.

"What are you thinking about, Robin?" Eleanor asked, caressing one of the paint-smudged arms crossed over her shoulders.

"That you're going to have a wonderful time. That you and Curly are going to be happy together," she replied.

"I knew you'd come around and accept him," Eleanor commented, smiling.

"I more than accept him. I like him a lot."

"Did you hire a detective to investigate his past? To make sure he was on the up-and-up, not a fugitive from justice?"

The question stung Robin to the quick. She almost blurted out, I would never do that to anyone! But she couldn't make such a righteous claim...not anymore. "I wanted to, when you first told me about him," she admitted.

Eleanor patted her arm. "Did I tell you what Caroline said in her letter to me? The one that was in the box with the kimono?" she asked.

"Nope. What'd she say?" Robin stood up and walked around the chair to face Eleanor.

"'Thank you.' That's all. Just 'Thank you.'"

Robin grinned. "Well, you did do a good job with me," she boasted, tossing her hair back and jutting her chin out proudly. "I can paint a room like a pro."

She got back to work, applying paint to a wall with careful brush strokes. With some measure of contentment, she listened to Eleanor talk of plans for her trip with Curly.

IN THE COMING WEEK Robin nearly finished painting the rooms of her house. By the time she saw her mother and Curly off at the airport on a Wednesday afternoon, there was only her bedroom left to be done.

Robin went back to the nursery after seeing them off. She noticed a rental car in the lot. It was not an ordinary sight, because Las Vegas was a taxi town. Visitors usually went from the airport to the strip and back to the airport, exploring the town no further than that.

Robin was pleased, always glad when people from out of state came to Eagle Garden. That kind of patronage meant that the nursery's reputation was widely spread.

She went into her office. Suzanne, the college student who worked part-time, came in. "There's only one customer and I've waited on him," Suzanne reported. "Did your mom and Curly get off all right?"

"Departure was on the button. Go on back in there and talk him into buying a *calibanus hookerii*, Suzanne. Nobody seems to want them, and they're taking up too much room. If you can unload one, I'll owe you a lunch."

"I'll try!" Suzanne said enthusiastically.

Robin left her office, going to the huge propagation room in which customers could discover, among many rows of plant-laden tables, some of the most unusual succulents in the world. Her back was to the door when she heard it open. She didn't look up from her work, assuming Suzanne or the customer, or both, had come into the room.

"Robin, hello."

She whirled, so stunned that she had to grasp the edge of a table for support. Jay was three tables away from her and had spoken softly, but she knew at the instant of the first syllable who had uttered her name.

His look was solemn. His golden hair was slightly tousled and his pants were creased from long-distance traveling. He was wearing a tan wool tropical suit with a pale pink shirt. His tie was awful.

"I'm buying this to give to you," Jay said.

The plant he held was potted in an unglazed clay chicken. There were several of those in the shop; animal pots were popular with customers. If any panda plants had been potted in clay doves, though, Robin would have given them away to charity.

Robin was too shocked to respond. Her nostrils were very slightly flared, and, just as slightly, her lips were parted over clenched teeth. Her hand maintained its frozen grip on the table edge. As if it had been mere days ago that they had parted rather than weeks, and as if the parting had been amicable, Jay blithely continued to talk about the plant he was holding.

"Caroline told me that you didn't take the first one home with you. I wanted to make sure you had one for your breakfast nook."

"I don't want one for my breakfast nook," Robin got out after inhaling a deep, jagged breath.

He shrugged. "Well, maybe on your nightstand, if your bedroom gets good light."

She shook her head at the impossibility of this situation. How could he startle her in this way, and then glibly make a joke of it? And this wasn't the contrite Jay who had sadly begged for forgiveness on the night she'd learned about the investigation. He didn't look contrite now.

"What do you want?" she snapped, not deigning to comment a second time on the plant.

"Oh, I came to do a little gambling. And, as I said, to replace the plant you left behind."

"Not funny."

Jay cocked his head and regarded her, then looked down at the plant and flicked a speck of soil off a fleshy leaf. "I don't mean to be funny, just as I didn't mean to be funny when I bought the other . . . what do you call this? The koala plant?"

Robin scowled and remained silent.

"Right, the koala plant. I bought the other koala because it was appropriate, what with the planter being a dove. However, this one is even more appropriate, if you stop and think about it."

He didn't elaborate, so Robin asked scornfully, "Are we back to witty bird references?" Primarily, her scorn was for herself, and consequently she seethed with resentment toward him. Jay had caused her so much grief, and yet she was glad to see him. She was so glad to see him that her knees had turned to jelly, requiring her to keep holding the table. The lack of self-control made her furious.

Jay met her words scorn for scorn. "Not a bit. I don't even think of a chicken as a bird, although it certainly is one. A gallinaceous one, if I remember my high school biology correctly. No, this is just symbolic, like I said. You know what the word chicken connotes, don't you? If you think the answer is that chicken is slang for fearful, cluck with pride, Robin, because you're right."

"I'm not afraid of you, Jay!" she flung at him. "You did something rotten to me, but you're not going to hurt me again!"

He put the plant down on a table. "No, I'm not," he said. "But you are afraid. You're afraid of men, because men—beginning with your two fathers—have hurt you. One didn't stay around to know you, and the other died when you were very young and needed a dad. Then there was the gambler."

"You're forgetting the football player in college, or didn't your investigation reach back that far!"

she cried in fury. That little lecture had done it. Her knees were just fine now, and she didn't have to hold on to the table for support. She stood tall and shoved her hands into her jeans pockets.

"No, it didn't go back that far," he said sharply, his eyes narrowed with anger.

"How far back did it go?" she demanded.

"It doesn't matter. And forget that damned investigation. I'm not interested in it anymore. It was a mistake, but it's history."

"Oh, well, one person's history is another person's fresh news." There was so much exaggerated disdain in Robin's tone that it tasted like bile in her mouth. "It was history to you even before I got to Hawaii," she said. "But it's still news to me, Jay. I didn't know about it until fairly recently. Of course, if it had been up to you, I wouldn't have known about it at all."

"Okay. I screwed up twice, first in spying on you and then in not telling you about it. But it's over. It is *over*, Robin. Stop using something from the past as a weapon against the future."

"Your keeping it secret told me a lot about the future, if I happened to spend it with you. It told me that if there were ever something terribly wrong, something that I should know about, I would be the last one told. It told me I couldn't ever trust you!" Robin cried.

"Rubbish," Jay scoffed. "That investigation was a convenience for you. It saved you from having to search for a genuine reason to run away from me, from us. The future scared you and you ran so you wouldn't have to contend with it."

"There is no us! There is no future for *us* to contend with! If you think there is, you contend with it by yourself."

Tears stung her eyes, tears that she didn't want him to see. She began to brush past him, muttering, "I've got work to do. Stay and shop all you want. Suzanne will help you with your purch—"

Her voice was stilled because he was kissing her. He had swept her off her feet and was kissing her and clutching her to him fiercely. Before she realized what she was doing, she kissed him back, but that only lasted a second. She clutched his arms harder than she ever had in sensuous passion, and pushed him away. When her mouth was free, she snapped, "How dare you think that a kiss solves everything. You think that I can forget what you did to me? That my life was scrutinized? I was stalked like an animal! My life was kept in an office file! It's probably still in one! I'll never understand how you could have done that to a person, not even to a stranger. I . . ."

"What?" he asked, when the barrage ceased. "You what? Hate me? Get it all off your chest. Say it all." She'd let go of his arms. Her furious grip on them had left wrinkles in his jacket.

Robin stared at him, realizing why she hadn't been able to go on with her last sentence. She'd been saying that she could never understand how he could do such a thing to someone. She put a hand over her mouth, shook her head lightly, then laughed. It was a short, breathless laugh. "I...Jay, I..."

"Robin?" He looked concerned, as anyone might who'd just witnessed someone go from rage to laughter.

She laughed fully now, shaking her head as if in disbelief. "I almost did the same thing to someone else," she confessed, still chuckling. "I almost had the man my mother is in love with investigated. I wanted his whole life laid bare before me so I could examine it for flaws!"

He wasn't smiling, and now his look was stern. "Robin, life was miserable without you." He said it almost angrily, almost desperately.

"I know. It hurt me, too, being without you," she whispered.

He took her in his arms again. This time, when she clung to his arms, Robin wasn't pushing him away. She held him to her and moaned against his mouth, and he was saying that she must never leave him again. She couldn't answer because he was kissing her again, but that was all she wanted. She didn't think she could ever be kissed enough.

She ran feverishly yearning hands over his shoulders, his back, his arms. She buried her fingers in his hair, but only momentarily, needing to explore his body more, to welcome it home to hers.

"I love you. I love you," she moaned softly. "Forgive me for hurting you, for letting you think I stopped loving you. I didn't, not for a minute. I've been so tormented. Jay, oh, Jay, darling, I couldn't stop loving you and it scared me."

"I know. I was scared, too, afraid that I wouldn't get you back. But we don't have to be afraid anymore. Oh, Robin, my beautiful, sweet Robin. Don't ever leave me again."

She held him tightly, reveling in the throbbing desire that moved her body in sensuous rhythm. She kissed him. She clung to him.

"Oops." Suzanne stood awkwardly in the doorway for a second, then quickly backed out, closing the door behind her.

"That was Suzanne," Robin explained.

"Do you want to introduce me to her as your fiancé, or should we let her think that you're engaging in a new sales technique?" he asked playfully.

When Robin didn't answer, Jay said softly, "This is the second time I've asked you to marry me, Robin. Do you need so long to make up your mind?" He kissed her lightly and added, "If you say yes, I'll take you home and ravish you. If you say no, I'll take you home and ravish you twice, and then you'll say yes."

"Then the answer has to be no," she said, between small sweet kisses. "I know a good offer when I hear one."

"Let's go," he said, first placing his hands on her shoulders and then gliding them down her arms.

Thrilled to the marrow, Robin didn't try to hide desire's effects on her. Shivering, she laughed and said that it was a ten minute drive to her house, that maybe she should clear off one of the propagation tables instead.

Jay hugged her. "Keep that winning attitude," he murmured after planting a kiss on her ear.

ROBIN WAS PROUD of her house. The builder had called it a garden home, which was a euphemism for small, but it was lovely and had a splendid mountain view.

"You're my first guest since I've redecorated," she said, then added almost shyly, "I did it myself. All the walls were a sort of Navaho cream color before. Nice, but plain. There's just the bedroom to be painted, and then I'll be done."

Jay looked around the living and dining areas. "It looks great. You've added to the resale value by painting, except that it's harder to sell a house that doesn't have neutral colors. Now you'll have to find a buyer who likes a lot of blue. But we don't have to worry about that right now." He came to her and placed his hands on her face, saying, "When *our* house needs painting, blue will be fine with me."

Robin was torn. On the one hand, she wanted to wait until after they'd made love before telling him she couldn't move away. On the other hand, she wanted to be honest with him, so that later he wouldn't have cause to feel he'd been deliberately misled. She weighed the choices and opted for honesty first, lovemaking second, even though it might mean she wouldn't end up in his arms at all.

"Jay, I'm not going to sell the house. I can't move to Hawaii," she blurted out. "When I was there I pretended to myself that I could talk Eleanor into retiring to Oahu. But she wouldn't do it, especially not now that she's in love. She wouldn't leave Curtis—Curly."

"Let's see the master bedroom," he answered noncommittally.

That surprised her. Flustered by his putting the dread topic off, she answered, "It's a mess. The furniture's all shoved together in the center of the room, with plastic all over it."

"Do you have a guest bedroom?" he inquired.

Wordlessly, Robin took his hand and turned toward the hall entrance. But after taking a step, she changed her mind about where to lead him. She turned around and circled Jay's neck with her arms and stood on tiptoe to kiss him. "I love you so much, Jeremiah Lasalle, that I want to make love to you on my own bed. That's very important to me."

They held each other for a moment, there in the freshly painted hall, and each explored with yearning fingers the loved one so sadly missed over the past month.

"We're not going to get to any bed," Jay prophesied in a loving murmur, slipping a hand under her knit top.

Eventually, though, they managed to move into the bedroom. Jay took the plastic sheet off the jumble of furniture.

Robin lifted two framed paintings she'd removed from the walls that morning off the bed. "I was going to paint tonight, and sleep in the guest room," she said, turning back the comforter and top sheet.

"This is a beautiful bed," Jay said. "Since you're obviously partial to it, we'll ship the whole thing to Hawaii."

Robin plunked herself down on the bed in dejection. "Jay, I *can't* go to Hawaii."

"Why not?" He started to remove his tie. "Tell me, Robin." He pulled the tie off.

She looked at him with disbelief. Apparently he was planning to undress and stand there in all his glory, while she tried to articulate her refusal to abandon her handicapped mother. He unbuttoned his shirt. "I don't know how to make you understand my position," she began, gazing at his beautiful and very virile chest.

"Try to make me understand," he said, pulling off a shoe. When his shoes and socks were off, he stood and put his hands on his belt. Robin sucked in a deep breath, anticipating. But he stopped and looked down at her without undoing the buckle. Go on, Robin—tell me what you think I won't understand."

"It's a difficult topic," she said distractedly. Her gaze traveled upward to his throat where she loved to nuzzle. And to his mouth, which could melt her completely.

"It'll get easier. Why don't you take your clothes off while we talk," he said.

Robin didn't feel like talking, and now she didn't feel like undressing, either. But deciding the latter was preferable, she sat up and took her sneakers and sports socks off, then pulled her top over her head. Her lace bra fastened in front, and she had that off in another second. She heard Jay's intake of breath and felt his eyes on her breasts, but he didn't say a word.

Without getting up from the bed, she undid the snap of her jeans, but then she couldn't go on. How were they going to make love, when a problem as vast as the land and sea separating Oahu from Las Vegas loomed ahead of them?

She left her jeans on and flopped back on the bed, her legs dangling off the side.

Jay was suddenly leaning over her, one knee resting on the bed between her legs. His balled fists sank into the mattress at either side of her head. With a quick sidelong glance, Robin saw the strength that sculpted one of the tanned arms that held her captive. His amber eyes lingered on her breasts, then met and locked with her gaze. "If, after we examine the pros and cons of your moving to Hawaii, you're absolutely certain that you can't, then you won't. I'll live here," he said simply.

She turned her head to the side, unable to meet his eyes. What he'd just said was ludicrous, and meaningless. It was a grand gesture of the moment and would have no impact on reality.

"Robin, look at me." Jay gently turned her face with one strong hand so she would have to meet his gaze. "I can't live without you. I don't have to spend my life in Hawaii, I have to spend it with you. You can't give me one good reason why we shouldn't be together."

"Lasalle Engineering," she said slowly.

"Lasalle Engineering can go on without me or even be moved here. There are all sorts of options. I don't need to head my own firm; my ego isn't that inflated. And believe me, if I'm not running my own show I'll be eminently employable." He dipped his head down and kissed one taut nipple, as if putting a seal on his words and ending the argument.

Robin writhed as he kissed the other nipple, then she said in a husky voice, "Caroline."

He finished the slow, tongue-flicking, playful kiss before answering. "I'm old enough to leave my stepmother."

"You hate Las Vegas," she whispered.

"Not anymore, I don't. Not now that I love one of Las Vegas's own. I'll find a lot of things to like in this town. What's the name of the mountain this house faces? It's gorgeous. I'm already crazy about it."

She'd always known the mountain's name, but she was so overwhelmed by what Jay was offering and so enflamed by his touch that she honestly couldn't remember. Her eyes prickled and there was a lump in her throat. She wanted to weep at his enormous generosity, but more than that she wanted to make love to her perfect man.

"Jeremiah, the only mountain I'm aware of is the mountain of feeling inside me. Its name is love. Would you please do me a big favor? Pull my jeans off—fast."

He took them off by inches, kissing the satin bareness of her as he uncovered each shapely inch. His lips and tongue left a trail of thrills down to her knees, but from there on down she was dangling over the side of the bed, so he quickly shucked the jeans the rest of the way off. He lifted her feet and, bending her legs gently, placed her toes against his slender taut belly.

He hadn't removed his slacks and belt yet, and he glided one small set of pink-nailed toes over his belt, from the buckle to his side, and then back to the middle. He then lifted those toes to his lips to be kissed, after which, while rubbing her ankle against the side of his jaw, he asked, "Are you ready to be ravished by a potential resident of the State of Nevada?"

"SUNRISE," Robin murmured against Jay's chest. Her face moved with his slow peaceful breathing. Sated and serene, she was lying on top of him and had been wafting in and out of a dream state for the past ten minutes. She felt so peaceful, so contented, and then she remembered she hadn't told him the name of the mountain.

"Mmph?" He sounded as though he were in a dream state himself.

"The mountain. Its called Sunrise Mountain. That's a lovely name, isn't it?"

In answer, he caressed her back with infinitely gentle strokes of his fingertips. Neither of them spoke for a few minutes, and then Robin murmured, "You must be tired from traveling and dealing with a stubborn woman . . . and then dealing with her again when she turned shamelessly lusty. Would you like me to fill the bathtub for you?"

"Will you get in it with me?" he asked quietly.

She nodded yes against his chest.

"Good, we'll do that after I sleep for a few minutes."

For the fifteen minutes he slept, Robin spent every second feeling grateful for being able to touch him as he lay there. Her heart beat to the rhythm of his breathing.

"NOW SAY you'll marry me," Jay commanded.

They were facing each other in the bathtub, Robin's toes tucked cozily under the sides of his hips. "Come on. Surely you wouldn't sit in a small bathtub with a large man unless you intended to marry him. It wouldn't be proper."

"I am feeling a little lascivious," Robin admitted, wriggling her toes. "But wasn't that the deal we made at the nursery? You would have to ravish me twice in order to get a promise of marriage?"

He shifted his position, leaning toward her.

"Jay! Not in here! We can't!"

He settled back against the end of the tub and the wall again. "Say it," he said.

Robin rubbed one foot and ankle against the outside of his thigh.

"Don't tell me with body language, honey," he advised. "I want to hear it."

"Jay. . ."

"No, don't start a conversation. Just say yes. You won't have to go to Hawaii if you don't want to."

"It isn't that I don't want to go," she said softly. "It isn't that at all. And I don't want you to leave your company, or move it here."

She thought about that for a moment, envisioning all Jay's employees telling their shocked families that they were moving to Las Vegas, Nevada. She giggled.

"What's funny?"

"Until your staff became acclimatized, you wouldn't be able to keep them out of the casinos. Jay, seriously, you couldn't move the firm here. It wouldn't work."

"I'm not worried about it," he insisted.

She heard the honesty that made the simple statement a gift to her. Of course she couldn't accept such a sacrifice on his part; it wouldn't be fair. Lasalle Engineering was too large a part of Jay's life to be forfeited, even for love. Robin asked herself if she could walk away from Eagle Garden. Didn't she love the business that had been a part of her life since her teen years? Even while she was in school she had worked in the nursery, always realizing that one day she would run it.

"Are you daydreaming while I wait to hear my fate?" Jay asked.

"Yes. I'm thinking of what it would feel like not to have Eagle Garden anymore. To be your wife. To live in paradise, with a perfect man. To . . ."

"To what?" he asked in a low, sensuous tone, grinning, clasping both her ankles and giving her legs a little shake.

"To eat your *laulau*," she replied with a laugh. "What did you say the ingredients were?"

"Butterfish, pork, taro and ti leaves."

"Mmm, sounds delicious. Yes."

"Yes?"

"Yes! Jay, yes! And...I'll—" She was going to tell him she would leave Las Vegas, would live her life in Hawaii, but he interrupted, saying, "Get in my arms, woman!"

"How? I . . . Oh, wait, let me—"

It was only water. The walls above the ceramic tile surrounds could be wiped dry. The carpet could be dried out. She was cradled against him finally; he was kissing her. "You're right, I shouldn't have painted all the rooms blue," she said between kisses. "Do you think I'll get a buyer?"

"I think you'll get a cold," he said, after kissing her again. "The water's tepid and you're starting to turn blue yourself. Come on, I'll dry you off."

As he did, Robin told herself that it would be all right, that Eleanor would be able to manage without her and would even live happily without her only child nearby. The trouble was, she didn't believe a word of it.

JUST AS ELEANOR HAD MET Robin alone when Robin returned from Hawaii, Robin went to the airport without Jay on the afternoon that Eleanor and Curly were due in from New Orleans. Eleanor had not sprung Curly on Robin too suddenly; she wanted to accord her mother the same consideration.

Jay not only agreed to stay behind, but he insisted on being useful. Robin's past few days had been so full—with loving Jay, popping into the nursery at all hours, introducing Jay to friends, showing him the nongambling side of Las Vegas and taking him to nearby Lake Mead and Boulder Dam—that her bedroom still hadn't been painted. Today, thanks to Jay, it would be.

Robin planned to spend the entire afternoon with her mother. Sometime during the day she would find the right moment to spring her big news. She hoped she could have Eleanor to herself for a while. Her upcoming move to Hawaii would have an impact on Curly's life, also, but she wanted first to discuss it with Eleanor alone.

Later, if Eleanor and Curly weren't too tired from traveling, they would be Robin's and Jay's guests for dinner at Liberace's. The restaurant was as dazzlingly cheerful as the great entertainer who had built it, and it served consistently good fare. The dinner would be a celebration of at least one engagement, and Robin had her fingers crossed that there would be another forthcoming marriage to toast with champagne.

Eleanor was the first passenger off the plane, and Robin discovered that she needn't have worried about having her mother to herself. She was stunned when she saw Eleanor carried down the steps without Curly right behind her. After they hugged and kissed, Eleanor said, "Let's not talk about it right now. Wait till we're in the van."

Robin felt ill, but as they waited for the suitcases she refrained from asking about Curly. To help the seemingly interminable minutes pass, she wanted to make small talk about the nursery, but she couldn't.

When they were inside the van, Eleanor didn't make Robin wait for an explanation of Curly's absence. "Curly is married," she said in a quiet, even tone.

Robin went white and she stared at her mother in horrified disbelief, while Eleanor told her the whole story. Curly had married a Savannah woman after a brief romance when he was stationed in Ft. Stewart, Georgia. They weren't suited to each other and soon parted. Curly was transferred to Washington and had no contact with his wife, but neither filed for divorce. Curly didn't mind remaining legally married if she didn't mind, because he didn't expect to ever want to marry again.

"Robin, you were right," Eleanor said, after explaining Curly's marital status. "He did pop the question. We were in a lovely restaurant, having a late supper. We'd come from hearing some of the sweetest Dixieland ever played, and we were both very happy with life. It was after I said yes that he told me he was still married to someone he hadn't seen in years and years. He said he'd file for a divorce immediately, and while we wait for it to be granted we can consider ourselves engaged to be married."

"Well...that's wonderful! But where is he now?" Robin asked. "Why didn't he come back with you?" Even though Curly's absence was perplexing, Robin felt much better already. In the airport she'd thought that Curly had abandoned Eleanor in New Orleans, and a few minutes ago she'd pictured a wife and children whom Curly had abandoned before coming to Las Vegas and entering Eleanor's life.

"He's not here because he went to see his wife. He didn't want to, but I insisted. We can't get married or live together until he's divorced, and I don't want him to get a divorce without discussing it with his wife. Between you, me and the lamppost, Robin, he wants to marry me so much that he said we could get married now, without anyone being the wiser. I appreciated the sentiment but told him I'm not going to be an accomplice in bigamy."

"But you don't have to get married!" Robin protested. "You can just go on being together, sharing your lives. Curly can still move in with you. The main thing is that you love each other. You mustn't let anything keep you apart."

"Do you mean that it wouldn't bother you if Curly and I lived together, even though he was married to someone else?"

Robin didn't need two seconds to think about it. "No, it wouldn't. Your living together won't hurt that woman."

"It would hurt me," Eleanor said. "I would think about her all the time."

"Mom, she might not even be alive! You and Curly are deserving of happiness. You're two good people who need, want and love each other. Those feelings can't be put aside until a piece of paper says that Curly is divorced and free to marry. He's been divorced, in his heart, for a long time. *That's* the divorce that matters."

"I wish I felt that way about it, but I don't," Eleanor said. "I'm having trouble with his having kept a secret from me at the beginning of our relationship. I can forgive him for that, because he's been wonderful to me in every way, but I wish we hadn't started out with a lack of honesty."

"If you can forgive him, and if you love each other, the battle's won," Robin said, thinking of her own recent experience.

"I can forgive, but what I can't do, unfortunately, is live with another woman's husband. To my mind it's the legal decree that makes a person divorced, not what's in his heart. So I told him that he'll have to be divorced before he can move in with me. And I don't want him to just file for a divorce and wait for it to be granted. I want him to see her, tell her face-to-face that he wants a divorce. No matter how little the marriage meant to both of them, it was a marriage. Vows were taken. So that's why he isn't here. He thought I was being silly— about his having to see her to tell her he wanted a divorce—but he didn't put it off. He rerouted and went to Georgia. He'll call me tomorrow. I just hope he doesn't have trouble finding her after all this time."

"I can't believe you did that," Robin said. "I can't believe it. You had him. You were all he wanted. And you sent him back to her. It's incomprehensible."

"No. It's ethical."

Robin sighed and sank back against the van's seat. There was no sense in arguing over ethics. But who would have thought that so soon after meeting Curly Gibbs she would find herself longing for him to be a part of her family, legally or not, for the rest of his life? "When we meet at the airport, you do give me big news," she said softly. "Mom, I hope you didn't blow it."

"Well, Robin, if there's a chance that they'll take one look at each other, swoon with longing and fall into each other's arms, then it's a good thing that I did send him back to her. But I'll admit that it was very hard for me when we said goodbye. He'd been disappointed in my attitude, and he's certainly not used to having a woman tell him what he must do. I think he expected me to chide him a little for misleading me in the beginning, and then say that everything was hunky-dory and we wouldn't give it another thought. He didn't expect me to insist he go looking for his wife. I just wanted to have enough courage to send him to her, to let him do the right thing."

Robin didn't think Eleanor had done the right thing, and she said so emphatically. "When he calls, I think you should tell him how much you love him and that he should come back and move in immediately. Whether the divorce takes a month or six months to be granted."

"Well, darling, despite my big adventure, my daring to have a love affair, I'm still a product of my generation and my upbringing. I can go so far, and no further. Are you really worrying that I'll lose him?"

"Mom . . . yes!" Robin hated to be this honest, because her opinion could be interpreted as a reflection on Eleanor's desirability as a woman. And that wasn't what she wanted to do. She tried to explain the gloomy prognosis she'd been compelled to utter. "It's not that I think he doesn't love you a lot—I *know* he does. But Curly's been a free spirit for a long time. He hasn't had to answer to anyone except himself. Being away from you and on his own, even for a short while, might make him feel that he misses the old vagabond life."

"Well, I'd rather have him discover that he misses it now than later, when we'd already married. Maybe that will happen. Maybe he won't marry me. Whether he does or not, I'll go on. I have Eagle Garden and my daughter. For a lot of years, that's been enough to keep me happier than most people are, and it'll go on keeping me just as happy."

So much for my moving to Hawaii, Robin thought grimly. Eleanor had spoken her feelings plainly. She had Eagle Garden and a daughter to keep her going.

Cheerfully, Eleanor went on, "Her name is Rita. She's probably sloppy about her appearance and a lazy housekeeper. Curly will take one look at the mess and thank his lucky stars that he has me."

Robin, on the other hand, pictured Rita as a seductive blonde who probably wore a black satin teddy to clean house in. She would be the kind who could slip sexily into old age without having one wrinkle on her face or dimples on her thighs. When Curly found her, she would open the door of her immaculately clean and sensuously decorated home, see him, sink to her knees and murmur throatily, "Thank you, Lord."

As she drove Eleanor home, Robin wondered if they would ever see Curly again. What would happen if they didn't? She envisioned herself asking Eleanor to move to Hawaii, to be near her and Jay. She couldn't do it. It would be tantamount to saying, "You're dependent on me. You need me. You have to give up all that you know, and your main interest in life, in order to be near me."

She would not insult her mother like that. But if Curly didn't come back—and if she married Jay and Eleanor didn't come to Hawaii with them— Eleanor would be alone. Jay was willing to live here, or he thought he was, but Robin knew that that would never work out.

"Let's not dwell on my problem," Eleanor said. "Tell me everything that's gone on since I left. How does your house look? Have you made any other changes?"

Robin pictured Jay, peacefully painting the pretty garden home that he thought was going up for sale soon. Her heart sank. If she couldn't keep her promise to him, how much damage would she have done? And how could she live without him, or live with herself after hurting him?

"I haven't had time to do anything else," Robin said guardedly. "We've been busy at the shop. Pat's back. She feels great. A third-grade class in Boulder City is coming on a field trip next week, and Suzanne got the idea of giving the children a choice of *peperomia asperulas* or *columellas* in two-inch pots to take home. We've never let kids choose their plants before, and I think that's a very good idea. I got a letter from Keith. He says being in the clinic is hard, but worth it, and he's sure he'll go the distance. He sounded very optimistic. I think there's already been a lot of progress toward his recovery."

"Wonderful! I think talking with you helped him make the decision to commit himself. You should feel very good about that, Robin."

At that moment, Robin despaired of ever feeling good about anything again. But yes, it was wonderful that Keith was finally dealing with his illness. When he'd asked her to have dinner with him, shortly before she went to Hawaii, she'd agreed to only because he'd told her he was trying to work up the courage to commit himself to a mental health clinic where he could be cured of his compulsive gambling.

Over dinner he'd asked if she might give him another chance, when he came back. She answered that it was too late for that, that she had no feeling left for him other than a hope that he would get well and lead a good life.

She'd said, "Go to the clinic, Keith. Eventually you'll find someone to love, but your first goal has to be to get well."

Then they'd drunk a toast to the future. It was at that moment their picture had been taken by the investigator.

Robin drove up the driveway of Eleanor's home. Eleanor surprised her by saying, "Have you heard from anyone else? Jay, for instance? Despite the fact that I didn't know what went wrong between the two of you, I've hoped every day since you told me about him that he would try to make things right."

Robin looked at her mother for a long moment, then folded her arms on the steering wheel and rested her head on them. "Jay is here." She sighed, still resting on her arms, but turning to face Eleanor. "He's at my house, painting my bedroom. He can't wait to meet you, so we were planning to take you and Curly to Liberace's tonight. Mom, please, when Curly calls tell him you miss him and want him to come back right away. Tell him we need him at the nursery, which we do. But more important, tell him you love him, that you want him to move in and share your life. Your living together won't be immoral."

Eleanor stroked a lock of Robin's hair, then moved it off her face so she could caress Robin's cheek with a fingertip. Her fingers were roughened from years and years of working with plants. "I suspect that when a man travels a great distance and then paints a woman's bedroom for her, he either wants to share that bedroom or take the woman back home to share his. Which is it?" Eleanor asked.

"He's willing to do either," Robin answered.

"Marvelous! Congratulations! And, Robin, Curly's coming back here has nothing to do with your future." Her words were gentle but firm.

"Oh, but it does," Robin replied. She admired her mother's courage and her unfailing optimism, but didn't feel she could share it.

"You don't think I could be happy knowing you'd given up Jay because of me, do you? Shame on you for even considering it. Robin, if Curly were free to marry right now and had a very good reason for wanting to live somewhere other than Nevada, I'd be packing. I wouldn't stay behind to be with you. I love you very, very much, but I'd go with my man. Well, what do you say to that?"

Robin sat up straight and looked out the windshield. She took a deep breath, let it out, licked her lower lip and blurted out, "I say that we should both move to Hawaii, and let's not wait. Curly can make the move now, or later when he's divorced, or..." *Or not at all*, she thought, but she went on with her urgent plea. "Honest, Mother, Oahu is paradise! If you were there for just two days, I wouldn't have to sell you on it."

Robin stopped and dead silence followed. "That's what I thought you'd say," she admitted, but she smiled gamely for Eleanor's sake.

"Robin Alyse Eagle, I think that being in love has addled your brain. Why would I want to live in Hawaii?"

Because Eleanor sounded as if she honestly didn't know, Robin told her: "I'll be there."

"You? What are we going to do together in Hawaii? Are we going to sit on the beach twiddling our thumbs all day? If you get your way and I give up Las Vegas, which is all the paradise I need here on Earth, what in the world will I do with myself? Don't say I'd open a nursery, because you know how risky that is. Eagle Garden's reputation and success couldn't be duplicated on Oahu. And I love this crazy town. I've lived here all my life—fifty-eight years! Just because I said I'd move away to make Curly happy, it doesn't mean I'd do it for anyone else, including you."

"It was just a thought," Robin said wearily. "Come on. Let's take your things inside." She felt like a pushy child who had been properly bawled out.

After lifting the suitcases onto Eleanor's bed, Robin apologized. "Mom, I'm sorry if anything I said was insulting. I know you're independent and capable. Maybe . . . maybe I'm the one who's dependent. We've always had each other nearby, and I kind of like it that way."

"I like it that way, too," Eleanor said, and Robin could see she was fighting back tears. "But we can both live without. Now go home. Didn't you say that the most exciting man in the world was waiting for you in your bedroom? He must be pretty bored with nothing but a paintbrush to hold."

"That's no way for a woman of your generation and upbringing to talk," Robin admonished, kissing her mother's cheek. "I'm going to miss you an awful lot," she added, and then, as she saw Eleanor lose the battle against the first tears, she had to turn and hurry out of the house before her own fell.

Jay was outside on the patio, lying on the sturdy lounge and looking up at beautiful Sunrise Mountain.

"Don't get up," Robin said quickly, as she opened the sliding glass door. "I love you in that position," she murmured, plopping herself down on top of him.

"Ummph! Ahh, that's better," he said. "Did you see the bedroom?"

"Uh-uh. I was in too big a hurry to see you."

"Well, give me a kiss I'll never forget, and then go look at it. I need praise for a job well done. And there's something else for you to see in there."

Robin obeyed his first command, then reluctantly got up and went back inside.

The bedroom was faultlessly painted, and the "something else" that Jay had wanted her to see was on her dresser.

The unwrapped and empty Baccarat crystal perfume bottle was standing on an envelope. Robin turned the bottle slowly in her hands, noting that the stopper was a crown. Exquisite, it was deserving of being filled with the finest perfume or of being left empty and admired for its own beauty.

"Open the card," Jay said from the doorway.

Robin hadn't heard him come inside or through the hall. His eyes held the peaceful joy of a man who knows that he is filling his beloved's life with happiness. Robin feasted on his smiling face before pulling the stopper from the bottle. *I love you*, she said. *I adore you*, she told him, though no spoken word broke the perfect quiet.

She put the bottle down on the dresser and opened the envelope. The card didn't have any printed words, but to Robin's delight the picture was of a plump, woeful-looking toad. It wore a lopsided crown on its warty head.

"The drawing was done before you transformed me, of course," Jay said.

Robin chuckled and exclaimed, "I can't get over the likeness. It's as if the artist actually had you for a model." Then she opened the card and read what Jay had written.

My darling,
Because of your love I am the king of the world. I love you so much that location has no meaning to me. Wherever you choose for our home, I'll be fulfilled there. Unlike this crystal bottle, our love can't be shattered. It will endure and grow forever. That's my undying promise to you.

Your Jeremiah

Their kiss was sweet, with lips barely touching, but Robin felt the passion deep inside herself. She knew that she would never kiss Jay—never even give him a peck on the cheek—without being aware of that everlasting passion. "How did you find time to shop?" she asked, taking her hands from his shoulders and entwining them behind his neck.

"I turned out to be a fast painter, once I got the hang of it. I not only shopped, I did something else."

"What?"

"Gambled."

"You didn't."

"Did too."

"Jeremiah. You succumbed to temptation."

"Yep. And I won five dollars from a nickle eating one-armed bandit."

Robin chuckled delightedly. She was relieved that Jay had gambled and won; now he would like Las Vegas better and look forward to their frequent visits here.

"Then I played blackjack and lost fifty," he admitted, adding, "I'm never going to gamble again. I hate gambling."

Robin threw her head back and laughed.

"How are Eleanor and Curly?" Jay asked, after taking Robin's postural change as an invitation to nuzzle her throat. "Are we taking them out to dinner? I guess I can still afford Liberace's."

Robin told him about Curly's being married and Eleanor's refusing to live with a married man. "My mother's being a fool. Curly's the best thing that ever happened to her, at least since my father died, and what does she do? She sends him back to a sexy blonde bombshell who polishes the perfect nails on her smooth hands three times a week."

"How do you know that about her?" Jay asked. "Have you had her investigated?"

"No, of course not. Jay, don't laugh at me. Seriously, what if he doesn't come back?"

"He'll be back," Jay prophesied. He hugged Robin, then lifted her off her feet, turned in a circle and put her down on the bed. "Don't you see that we're able to joke about something that we once thought was an earthshattering problem between us? Your mother and Curly will joke about this problem, too."

He had lain down beside her and she now climbed astride him. "Mother shouldn't have made him do something he didn't want to do. This might really ruin their happiness. They aren't like us. They aren't—"

"They're not what?" Jay interrupted in a gentle tone. "Young? Madly in love?"

Robin repeated the questions to herself and answered them in silence. Young? Eleanor had looked younger when she left for New Orleans than she had in far too many years. Madly in love? Perhaps they were and perhaps they were not. Who could know, except Eleanor and Curly?

"Robin, let it be," Jay said gently. "Let your mother live her life without your pronouncing judgment on her future."

Robin sighed. Still astride Jay, she leaned down and kissed him. "You're so right," she admitted. "Jay, I want us to live our life in Hawaii. I've just been terribly hung up over leaving her. Underlying all my worries is the fear that she'll think she's second best because she's only my adoptive mother, that I'm choosing my birth mother over her."

"That's ridiculous. You're choosing me."

"I like the way you put that," Robin said. "Do you know what, Jay? Your optimism is infectious. From this moment on I'm going to have faith in all our futures, even Curly's. So why don't we go ahead with our plans for tonight, even without Mr. Gibbs. I'll call Mother and ask if she'll go out to dinner with us, to celebrate our engagement."

"That's the spirit. But first, since you're on top of me, I think I'll enjoy the most beautiful breasts in the world. And while I do that, why don't you give me a kiss I won't forget for as long as I live."

She leaned down. Jay softly cautioned, "Wait for my hands." She did, but just when they were getting involved in a very special kiss, the phone rang.

"Hmph?" Robin asked, then translated, "Should I answer it?"

Jay grunted back in the affirmative.

"Hello," Robin said, after reaching for the bedside phone. She looked down into her lover's eyes while listening to Eleanor's news.

Eleanor was so excited that Robin couldn't get a word in edgewise, except for an occasional, "Oh?" and "Hmm!" Jay's eyes, at the beginning of the call, had been half closed, revealing sensuous desire. Now they were wide open with curiosity.

Finally she was able to voice a complete sentence. "We're taking you out to a celebration dinner! Can you two be at Liberace's at eight?"

After hanging up the phone, Robin gave a delighted cry, and Jay winced when her bottom bounced on a vulnerable part of his anatomy. "Sorry!" she said, grinning. "Oh, Jay! Oh, darling! I'm ecstatic!" She started to bounce again, so Jay quickly grasped her hips to ease her descent.

"Obviously Curly's back," Jay surmised.

"He is indeed. He got to Savannah, looked in a phone book, found his wife, went over there, had coffee with her and her boyfriend, shook hands and went back to the airport. And incredibly he managed to get on the next flight headed for Las Vegas. Tomorrow he's going to file for his divorce, and then he and Mom are going to shop for a ring. He even accepts that he can't move in with her before the divorce. Oh, Jay, I'm so happy I can't stand it."

"I'm feeling a lot happier, too," Jay said, grinning widely. "Where's Curly staying tonight? Do you want to offer him the guest room?"

"That's sweet," Robin said, genuinely touched by the spontaneity of his generosity. "You're willing to give up our privacy tonight for my future stepfather. But he's got a better offer. Mom's compromising her principles, just for tonight, to celebrate."

Robin leaned down and whispered against Jay's ear, as if imparting a very wicked secret. "Did I ever tell you that Curly has three patriotic tattoos?"

He gripped her arms and pushed her up, his mouth open in righteous indignation. "No! Three? That's scandalous! It changes everything. Call her back and tell her we won't let her marry him."

Robin got off him and scrambled over to the edge of the bed. With glee lighting her eyes, she looked down on Jay's dear face as she picked up the phone.

"You wouldn't," he protested.

Robin puckered up and blew him a kiss. Then she called Liberace's and asked for a table for four. The gentleman taking the reservation asked if she were

Ms Eagle from Eagle Garden. He said he'd brought his mother in to the nursery two days ago, and she bought a *calibanus hookerii*.

In her happiness, Robin couldn't contain herself. "Yes, I own Eagle Garden, with my mother! We're both getting married! That's what tonight's dinner is for—to celebrate our engagements! Your mother will love her plant! Just tell her to be sure to water it thoroughly, and then let the soil dry out completely before watering again. Right, it's a winter grower. Oh, good, do bring her in again on her birthday! I'll be sure that she's given a complimentary gift from the shop. No, I won't be there . . . I'll be living in Hawaii. But my mother will continue to run Eagle Garden, with her husband."

Jay put a hand over his face and muttered, "I don't believe this is happening. She's telling her life story to a stranger."

Listening to the man offer both his best wishes and the best table in the restaurant, Robin grinned, shrugged a shoulder and winked at Jay. She was silently saying to him, This, honey, is the kind of news that makes everyone hearing it feel a lot happier. And so that one more person could share the happiness, Robin next dialed Caroline's number.

What readers say about Harlequin Temptation . . .

One word is needed to describe the series Harlequin Temptation . . . "Exquisite." They are so sensual, passionate and beautifully written.

—H.D., Easton, PA

I'm always looking forward to the next month's Harlequin Temptation with a great deal of anticipation . . .

—M.B., Amarillo, TX

I'm so glad you now have Harlequin Temptation . . . the stories seem so real. They really stimulate my imagination!

—S.E.B., El Paso, TX

Names available on request.

Harlequin Temptation

COMING NEXT MONTH

#141 LOVE IN TANDEM Lynda Ward

When Meredith first ran into Brandt, they were both stunned by the impact. Of course, she *had* knocked him off his bicycle. But what happened between them later was no accident....

#142 NO PASSING FANCY Mary Jo Territo

O'Mara was a man with fantastic moves, but Jo was the woman to show him a thing or two more....

#143 BED AND BREAKFAST Kate McKenzie

When Leslie O'Neill moved into the quaint but chaotic Seaview Inn, she suspected her stay would be less than serene. Already she was wishing her charming host, Greg Austin, would offer her more than bed and breakfast....

#144 TWELVE ACROSS Barbara Delinsky

Leah hadn't planned on being stranded in Garrick's secluded cabin. But she had no more control over the storm outside than the one that raged within.